Spirit of the

Shelley Davidow was born and grew up in South Africa. A nominee for the first Macmillan Writer's Prize for Africa in 2002, and the author of numerous books for children and young adults, she lives in the USA with her husband and son.

Shelley Davidow

Spirit of the Mountain

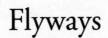

Flyways

First publication in English as *All Anna's Children*
by Tafelberg Publishers, Cape Town, in 1996
Published in 2003 by Flyways, an imprint of Floris Books

British Library CIP Data available

ISBN 0–86315–427–1

Printed in Europe

For Tim and for Paul,
with love

Chapter 1

It was the first day of the December holidays. The soft blanket of early morning fog enveloping Durban's city centre was already lifting. Emily held her breath and blocked her nose to avoid the traffic fumes as she crossed the main road to the Marine Parade. Through the confusion of noise and bustling people she could just hear the rumbling of the sea. Her face was already sticky with the thick subtropical summer air.

Hot cement burnt her feet and she pulled her peaked cap low over her eyes so that she would not see the homeless children on piles of newspapers, sleeping curled in the shadows of the steps that led down to the beach. But she saw them anyway, and her throat tightened. Two joggers ran by, young women. Their legs were perfect ... smooth and golden and slender. Emily glanced down at her own legs with distaste. She clenched her toes in the morning sand and blinked furiously, watching the waves tumble, muddy and brown, onto the glistening shore.

On her way back to the two-bedroomed flat that she shared with her mother, Emily stopped at the café. A fan creaked wearily from the ceiling of the small store, but did nothing to cool the place or keep the flies off the fruit. Emily found what she was looking for: *Reader's Digest* ... "Thin Thighs in Thirty Days!" She studied the picture of the girl on the front cover. She was very beautiful. Probably only a year or two older than Emily herself. She had long hair and clear, green eyes, lighter than her own. Her legs extended carelessly from her yellow shorts as if she was totally unaware of them, and had no idea how perfect they were. Emily bought a giant pack of Carefree gum.

She returned to a silent and empty flat. Her mother had left a note stuck to the mirror in the hall: "Back late. Macaroni cheese in the freezer. At Rodney's if you need me."

Emily sauntered through to the bathroom. Rodney was her mother's latest boyfriend. She had met him once and didn't like him. Still, if her mother was at Rodney's, it would make it easier to avoid dinner. She had skipped breakfast for the past two days, and that had been easy enough. If she stood on the bathroom scales at about 10am, not having eaten, she weighed just under 45 kilograms.

She stared at herself in the full-length mirror, at her short, reddish-blonde hair. The mirror seemed pleased with itself and she scowled at her reflection. Her cheeks were too round and made her look like a chipmunk, and her hips were too big for her body. If she stamped her foot she could count twenty wobbles of thigh-fat before it stopped moving. Twenty! Unbelievable. She stared at the reflection as though at a stranger. She shouldn't have cut her hair; it made her look like a sucked mango pip. Foolish, stupid, idiot thing to do. And surely that fat girl in the mirror couldn't be her!

december 8th
day one of december holidays — a saturday —
mom forgot my art class today maybe she
thought that holidays meant all activities of mine
would come to an end. it is now 11 in the
morning and i have eaten nothing yet. have given
up on punctuation wherever possible. i have to
confess that i have not yet had the guts to ask
whether i can spend the holidays on the farm
with uncle Tim. (he deserves a capital letter) and
now it already is december.

By four in the afternoon Emily's stomach was a knot of hunger. She sat at the desk in her room. A bright ray of sunshine fell across the paper in front of her. Outside the window the Durban traffic hummed and hissed and yawned like the waves on the beach. The stalls of the flea market were bright and colourful and reflected the afternoon light. She was sketching a pyramid in the desert, with the head and shoulders of the Pharaoh Tutankhamen looming above it, his blank eyes staring into the distance. Emily thought about the Egyptians. The dead pharaohs still influenced those who lived, she'd read. Even Anna believed that her own ancestors still had power over the living, cursing and blessing the people of their choice. Was it all a whole lot of make-believe, all this stuff about the power of other worlds? How could you know? As she drew, her mind turned over ways of asking her mother permission to go away to her uncle's farm.

Uncle Tim was just the opposite of her mother. She

was manicured and dainty, but he had rough, hard-worn hands and a thick beard, and it looked as though he had never brushed his hair, although he assured his sister that he had, at least once. Emily's mother didn't find Uncle Tim's personal habits or his unusual ideas amusing. He was a herb-enthusiast, and specialized in all sorts of mysterious home-grown tonics and organic remedies. "Overgrown hippy," Emily's mom would say. "Herbs and star signs ... I don't want you listening to him, Emily." But beneath it all she loved him. He was, after all, her brother, as well as being the most amiable human being on the face of the planet, the kind of man who could hug a porcupine and not feel its prickles, Emily always thought.

The last time that Emily and her mother had been to his KwaZulu-Natal farm, Emily had spent almost all her time with Anna. Anna was a Zulu woman, Uncle Tim's chief assistant on the farm. She knew more about his herbs and their properties than Uncle Tim did himself. For reasons Emily still couldn't fully understand, her mother had been furious that Emily had spent so much time with Anna. Matters had come to a head when her mom had caught her plastering her face with thick, reddish-brown mud. A face mask, she had tried to explain. Anna's idea.

She closed her eyes and remembered the farm, the smell of pine trees and porridge and cooking fires and herbs and honey, the sound of cocks crowing as the sun came up. She chewed the skin off the side of her thumb and frowned. She *would* go to the farm, even if it meant running away. Not that her mother would notice. Rodney was always there to fill up time and take up space.

Emily sat unseeing in front of the television set. She heard the door open and smelt the sweet, familiar scent of jasmine.

Her mother walked into the lounge. She'd done her blonde hair so that it looked thicker. There were dark rings beneath her eyes.

"How was your day, Emily?" She plonked herself down on their brown couch and sighed.

"Fine. Yours?"

"Oh, you know, exhausting. I'm sorry I haven't been home much lately." Her mother rubbed her forehead above her eyes and Emily looked away. She did seem tired.

"That's okay. You forgot my art class."

"Oh God, did I? I don't know how that slipped my mind!"

"It's okay," Emily said and looked out from beneath her fringe at her mother, who was pouring handfuls of dry, roasted peanuts into her hand and throwing them into her mouth. They hit the back of her throat with a dull, fleshy thud. Emily took a peanut and licked it. Then she took another and did the same, and another, until her hand was full of peanuts with the salt licked from them. She stood up. "I want to go to the farm for a few weeks," she said suddenly.

"What?" Her mother's voice was deceptively calm.

"Uncle Tim says I can spend as long as I like there. I want a holiday. Away from all the people and noise. Can I go?"

"Emily, you know how I feel. It's out of the question. Let's not argue about this, please!" Her mother leant forward and linked her hands over her slender, stockinged legs. She attempted to smile. "Please, Emily!"

Emily walked out of the room, stretching her sleeve over the hand holding the peanuts. She went into the bathroom, wrapped the peanuts in tissue paper and flushed them quickly down the toilet.

She lay awake that night. Her body felt shaky and she could not fall asleep. She imagined what it was like in the passages beneath the pyramids, imagined walking down the damp corridors of an ancient tomb, far from the city and the noise and the sad children on newspapers. In the tomb she was in the presence of some strange and ancient magic.

Suddenly a picture of Anna came to her — thin, tall Anna, Anna with her dark, hooded eyes, Anna with her slow, sure movements and her firm and gentle voice. Anna who walked with her back straight and her head held high, as though she were seeing something of which no one else was quite aware.

december 9th
i must be some kind of flipping genius. managed to not eat A THING while in my mom's ravenous presence. gave in this morning and ate an apple and a health-food bar. (oh dear oh dear). but ta DAH ... 42 kilos this morning. the measurement of my thigh area = still not that much different. (too gross a number to quote). i think i need to get to 38 kilos inordertobethesameas: magazine girl. yesterday uncle Tim phoned from kwazulu. he

*thinks it's a good idea that i go there. i told him
my mom's not that keen about me being
influenced by him and the farm people, that she's
afraid i'll become a tramp like him. he just
laughed.*

Emily woke with a churning stomach. She breathed in the fresh aroma of brewed coffee and wrapped her arms tightly around herself. She walked to the window. Far below her, vendors were selling fried bananas and pineapples at the flea market. Seagulls called shrilly in the humid morning air. She wondered about her metabolism. If you don't keep exercising, it slows down.

She found her mother at the breakfast table, poring over the *Natal Mercury* as she sipped dangerously strong coffee.

"I haven't seen you eating anything for the last while, Emily," her mother said to her coffee cup. Emily stopped in her tracks, startled.

"I eat all the time. I just wasn't hungry yesterday."

"Nonsense. I can see you getting thinner and thinner. That's not just from a day of not eating."

Emily looked down at the floor and curled up her toes. "I don't want to talk about it," she said softly. "It's not important."

"It *is* important," her mother said and ran her hand through her fluffy blonde hair. She glanced at her watch. "I have to go." She looked at Emily. "And you should get together with some of your friends from school. You spend too much time alone. I don't know why you're so antisocial."

"I'm fine, okay? I like my life as it is." Emily mustered a bright smile. "I promise, I'm fine. Really."

december 10th
it's midmorning and i have just eaten half a
packet of cashew nuts which is horrible. i don't
know what to do with myself. i am AWFUL for
stuffing myself like that. sis emily sis you
disgusting thing.

The next morning arrived cool and rainy, and the cars outside skidded and slid over wet streets. Emily woke with a light head. She could not move from her bed and her legs felt heavy. She could hear familiar noises in the kitchen as her mother made herself breakfast. Then she smelt the toast. The soft, wheaty aroma pulled her out of bed by her stomach.

"I'll be home early this afternoon from Rodney's," her mother said as Emily stumbled sleepily into the kitchen. "To take you to your art class." She wiped a loose eyelash delicately from her eyelid.

"Thanks. It's the last one anyway."

"Sorry that I forgot last time."

"That's okay. Mom?"

"Yes?" Her mother looked up and ran her tongue over her lips.

"Uncle Tim would really like me to spend the holidays on the farm. Can I go?"

"We've discussed it already," her mother said, her voice rising.

"But why? You can't just say no, just like that."

14

"You know that I don't like his ideas, and I don't like those people he has around him the whole time. I don't want you with them, I don't want you being influenced by them. And that's final."

Emily slapped her thighs in exasperation. "They're just like us," she argued. "Anna's a herbalist. What's wrong with that?"

"I don't want you with people who make *potions* and *muti* and consult with *witch doctors* and *medicine men* and whatever else they have up there. I don't want you with them."

Emily took a loaf of bread from the yellow bread bin. She tore off a hunk and stuffed it in her mouth. She could taste the grain. The feeling of food in her mouth made her stomach rumble and her saliva glands ache. Then she tore off another piece and another, swallowing the bread without chewing.

"For God's sake, Emily!" Her mother looked at her and shook her head. "You can't eat like that! Have a slice of toast, not a whole loaf of bread."

The bread stuck in Emily's throat and a fit of hiccups shook her. She banged her chest and went to the bathroom where she waited until her mother left the flat.

She found the box of herbal laxatives in the medicine cabinet. Two tablets once a day, the directions said. She took five and swallowed them dry.

december 12th
i have spent all day inside and radically
overdone the pyramid picture. it's close to ruin;

also i'm feeling dizzy and have a sore throat
(hope i'm not about to get some terrible disease)
... my mom is late as usual and hasn't phoned
so i guess she's spending time with rodney-the-
dog. (apologies) but all i've ever heard him say
is: it's a dog-eat-dog world (doesn't he know
that dogs don't eat other dogs?) nevermind.
hope that there is some way to get to the farm.
uncle Tim seems to think so. the noise of the
traffic is BLOWING MY MIND. *well, have dropped to*
41 and a half (congratulations) but ate rather a
lot today and will try not to eat so much again
EVER *in case it stretches my* FAT *stomach ... i*
wonder why my mom likes such young
companions, rodney's at least ten years
younger. hope that some MAGIC *changes her*
mind and that on christmas day i am
miraculously on the farm.

Her library book, *A History of Ancient Egypt*, lay open
on the lounge floor. She looked at the picture of a withered and dry skeleton-man, more than 5000 years old,
mummified and resting in a glass case in the British
Museum in London. He was emaciated. Only skin covered his bones. Bleached-blond hairs still stuck to the
top of his skull. His frame was small, like a child's, and
the skin was a dark, leathery brown. He seemed to be
lying in a defensive position, as if to protect himself.
Why had they brought this man from the place where
he had rested for so many centuries? He had existed on
the same continent on which she now lived. She looked

at the picture carefully. Then she took a piece of char-
coal and began sketching.

december 14th
art classes now over. yesterday was a waste of
time since i hate still life (how stupid to spend
hours drawing two apples and an orange in an
old basket!!) i now weigh just under 40 and need
to lose about two more. mom is threatening me
with a visit to our family doctor. she can do
what she likes — i look normal enough and
anyway there's nothing he can do about it.
mom's tense mood explained by the arrival of
new BOYFRIEND *— big and handsome and blond*
and a surfer. she saves all her good moods for
him (exit rodney-the-dog) i think i'll run an ad
in the paper: genuine doormat available
(human) will absorb all personal frustrations
and bad moods (me). uncle Tim phoned and said
not to worry he'll bring her around and i'll be
on the farm in no time.

Before sunset Emily went for a run along the beach.
The waves were loud and rough, crashing down onto
the shore as the tide came in. Across the sky streaks of
pink and blue stretched out to the end of the world.
The horizon was lit with a line of gold. She held her
dizzy head between her hands.

If you jog for half an hour you burn up about 300
calories, she'd discovered. That would burn a lot of fat,
especially if you only eat a yoghurt (120 calories) and

an apple (50 to 60 calories). Also, jogging raises your metabolic rate for several hours after you have finished, so if you run in the evening, you can go on burning fat during the night.

She wondered about the pharaohs, and about the afterlife and the ancestors and all that stuff about life and death. Was there really Something Out There that you couldn't see, Someone wiser than you who, for example, saw that you were only thinking about food? Who heard you counting calories, measuring your weight, who watched you as you looked at the fat wobbling around your thighs? How embarrassing!

She took off her cap and ran her hands through her hair. Her feet ached. She looked down at her thighs and grimaced.

evening
warren is a tall handsome plastic god whom i
never wish to see again. (emily how awful) ... i
hope my mom is happy. the picture of the 5000-
year-old man is not finished. its problem is that
it's dead. the drawing i mean. it's like i have no
energy. i can't even lift a pencil. i just want to
sleep and not do anything.

She was awake when her mother arrived home. The front door slammed. Her stomach churned and cramped. It was as if a knife were being twisted inside her. She was exhausted, but her eyes wouldn't stay shut.

midnight
i can't sleep and it's as if i am thinking about food
all the time. i think of what i would like to eat. ice
cream; a sandwich toasted with mayo and cheese
and everything; after that a bar of chocolate. there,
that's as good as having eaten it, isn't it? i am
dreaming of death, thought i knew what it was
like to be stabbed. is this normal for teenagers or
am i simply morose? answer freely in your own
time, ladies and gentles, or feel free to comment
LOUDLY at any time, if there is something OUT THERE
as the egyptians seem so sure of.

"Why aren't you eating anything, Emily?"

Emily pulled her fringe over her eyes and tapped her foot against the kitchen table. "I'm not really hungry, Mom."

"We have an appointment with Doctor Burns this afternoon."

"What for? Don't be ridiculous!"

"I've been watching you, Emily. I don't like your eating habits. And all my laxatives are gone."

"Mom, you're overreacting. I'm just on a sort of controlled-eating plan. I want to lose two more kilos, then I'll stop."

"But we're still going to the doctor this afternoon. Now eat your breakfast."

Emily looked up from the bowl. Her mother's dressing gown was yellow with pink flowers on the edges. It smelt faintly of smoke. She took the bowl of cereal and sighed.

"I'll be in my room," she said. In her bedroom she found a plastic shopping bag and emptied the milky cereal into it. She waited for enough time to pass, then returned the empty bowl to the kitchen and threw the bag into the dustbin beneath the sink.

The telephone rang and she heard her mother pick it up. Her heart lurched. She crept up to her mother's bedroom door and put her ear against the wood.

"Listen, Timothy," Emily heard, "this is a serious situation and I have no intention of letting her go to you in this state. No, of course I'll hear what the doctor has to say first. How do you think I feel? I've been on tranquilizers, dammit! God, Timothy, people die from this. Don't tell me to calm down, what do you know about parenting? I've done this all on my own, Timothy. You've no idea. It's affecting me so badly I can't sleep ..."

She didn't want to hear any more.

december 15th
both good news and bad news, ladies and you-know-whos. the bad: something rather ODD is going on. my mom is WORRIED about ME!!? i suppose maybe it's a little problem, not eating, but i just can't eat. just in case i stretch my stomach. the doc was great. at first i felt like running straight out of the waiting room. i told the doc i was fine and he asked me some questions, like are your periods regular? (how embarrassing!) then he asked my mom to leave us alone for a few moments. the good news: when she was gone he grinned at me as if the two of us

were in cahoots or something. *as if he knew he couldn't* MAKE *me eat. he asked me if there was anything i really wanted right now, or if anything was bothering me. so i said right out that i want to spend the holidays on the farm. and it's bothering me that my mom won't let me go. so he did it. it was that simple. he told mom to let me go. so it was a good move, going to the doc. imagine being stuck around* HERE *for a whole month of free days????*

Chapter 2

The green, rolling hills of KwaZulu-Natal unfolded
before them. Uncle Tim drove the truck with one
brown arm resting on the open window, his other hand
casually holding the wheel. His tatty farmer's hat hung
low over his eyes. His mouth was relaxed. He smiled
and looked fondly at his niece. "Happy now, City
Girl?" he teased.

"Oh, come on, I'm hardly a city girl!"

He laughed out loud. Could he really be related to
her mother? It seemed hardly possible. Ahead of them
the mountains grew larger, rockier. Thick mist
enfolded them.

"Is Anna there, Uncle Tim?"

"Yes, and she knows you're coming. She was glad to
hear that you were able to make it."

"Jeepers! I would have run away if it had come to
that!" Emily leant her head against the window. Uncle
Tim was so laid back he was almost horizontal. She felt
comfortable. It was a good feeling, an unusual feeling.
The road before them disappeared into mist and the
truck bumped over uneven tar. Emily took a deep
breath of clean, country air. Her head fell against the
door and she dozed off, listening to the hum of the
engine. Slowly, through watery dreams, the thin body
of the ancient man appeared. Before her eyes he grew
younger and younger, until he was just a child. He was

sleeping peacefully. She knew she should give this strange, withered child something to eat. He had not eaten for 5000 years and she could feel his hunger inside her own stomach. She brought a spoon of porridge to his shrivelled lips, but as she did so her own hunger grew so strong that she stopped the spoon in mid-air.

She awoke with a jerk as the truck rumbled onto a sand road. She licked her dry lips and Uncle Tim smiled. "Nearly there," he said. "Just another half-hour."

A soft drizzle began and the moist air seeped through the open window. It was fresh and smelt of wet soil and underbrush. Slowly, through the rain, the purple shadow of a mountain appeared. It was like the shape of a sleeping giant. She dangled her hand out of the window and felt the tiny droplets on her arm, clinging and cool.

"So, Em, what's it like being young in Durban at the beginning of a new century?" Uncle Tim asked.

Emily shrugged. "I suppose it's okay. Kind of like being on the cutting edge! What's it like being thirty-four on a farm at the beginning of the century?"

"Wonderful," he said enthusiastically. "Exhilarating. Have you forgotten? The beauty here, the magic, the smell of freshly baked bread, the roosters crowing in the morning ... and Anna boiling up magical potions for this and that. And of course you haven't met Joey."

"Joey?"

"I won't say more," he said with a twinkle in his eye.

"But I have lots of work lined up for you, if you have the strength. Seedlings need planting, herbs need sorting, and this time you should learn how to ride. I can't have a niece who's afraid of my horses. Feel up to it?"

"Anything, sir!" Emily laughed. A feeling of happy anticipation tingled through her.

The farmhouse appeared suddenly through the drizzle. The chimney was hidden in low cloud and the brickwork looked as solid and strong as ever. Cows lowed in the distance. Dogs barked and two alsatians came to growl half-heartedly at the approaching truck. Uncle Tim ground to a halt outside the house and she climbed out. The smell of wet grass made her think of the past.

When she was really small, before her father had left for England for ever with another woman, they had sat cosily together in the evenings in front of the log fire, listening to Uncle Tim tell about the snakes he had removed from the house, and the baboons that had once sneaked through the kitchen door and stolen jam and bread and finished Uncle Tim's cold coffee. In the mornings they would walk out together, her parents arm-in-arm, breathing out white puffs of mist in the crisp, damp air.

She shook her head and ran to the huge oak door, rubbing her arms. She dropped her bag on the veranda and looked back at Uncle Tim.

"Go in," he said. "Anna's waiting for you."

The wooden floors creaked in the entrance hall, and the familiar log fire crackled from the lounge.

She could smell the pine logs that fed the fire. She heard a clatter in the kitchen and gently nudged the door open.

Anna seemed taller than ever. She was wearing black boots and leggings. She had tied a red scarf around her head. Her hands were busy sealing packages of dried rosemary. Her smile reached her eyes and she dusted her hands on her thighs.

"Hey," Emily grinned.

"Hello," Anna said. Her face shone in the kitchen light. When she smiled, dimples appeared on her cheeks. She took a step towards Emily and embraced her, rocking her from side to side. Then she let go and her eyes travelled over Emily's body. "I want to say you look well," she said honestly, "but you don't."

"Oh, come on!" Emily replied. "I feel great. Those herbs smell incredible."

Anna smiled, opened the oven and pulled out a tray of steaming bran muffins. Their aroma made Emily feel faint. Uncle Tim arrived in the kitchen and put his hat down on the table.

"Well, Em, I suggest some coffee with our muffins, and then Anna can show you what needs doing," he said.

december 17th, 10pm
here i am and it feels as though i've gone from the future back into the past. all the smells of the farm and anna ... it's great. i feel so bad — had to flush one of anna's delicious muffins down the toilet — couldn't risk her being concerned or hurt

*by me refusing to eat ... i feel disgusting about
that ... and there has been violence (overheard
uncle Tim) in the township not even five ks from
here. all my art stuff is here which is good since
without it i really am nothing but a bundle of
bones and skin. (no lights on here and nobody
home if i don't have my crayons and paint and
paper) ... i am writing by candlelight. how
romantic, tho' i am not romantic in the least. it is
so quiet. just the noise of hyperactive crickets in
the thickets and frogs in the bogs on logs. ha ha.
goodnight.*

Soft dew on the wooden window frame caught the
early-morning light and a cock crowed in the distance.
Emily heard voices, strange, unfamiliar voices, deep
and loud. They were speaking Zulu. She was there on
the farm and it was morning and she was starving as if
she had not eaten in weeks. She slipped out of bed and
trod softly across the wooden floor. She opened the
door and tiptoed down the passage to the kitchen.
There was the faint aroma of coffee. Uncle Tim was
probably up and about already and busy on the farm.
The sun was right up over the horizon. Outside the
window she saw men in farm clothes talking loudly,
drinking out of tin mugs. They were laughing, their
faces shining. A cup of coffee. Emily went to the cup-
board and took a cup. The coffee tasted like thick,
gooey chocolate. Her stomach curled and seethed. She
had to take in a breath to stop her throat constricting.
"Morning."

She turned and saw Anna standing in the doorway. "Want some coffee?"

Anna shook her head. "Come, let me show you where I stay."

"Okay. Let me get some shoes."

She put on an old pair of blue trainers and followed Anna out into a dewy morning. The mountains surrounding the farm were invisible in the thick, low cloud. They walked over damp grass. The farm sloped gently to the west. A pathway emerged and they followed it to the end. She remembered that in this particular place there used to be a large circular water tank. Now there was a white rondavel with a thick, thatched roof and two doors.

"Sshh," Anna put a finger to her lips. "This door's Joey's. It's his day off. He's still asleep."

"Who's Joey anyway?" Emily asked, wrapping loose strands of hair behind her ear as Anna opened her door.

"Aha," Anna said and smiled enigmatically. Emily frowned. What was there to be so secretive about?

The door of the rondavel creaked open. The room was huge and semicircular. A thick rug covered the floor and lace curtains hung in front of the windows. The room was beautiful and fresh and bright.

"Bathroom's outside," Anna indicated. "This was the water tank, you know."

"I thought so," Emily said, her eyes travelling over the room.

"Yes," Anna grinned. "Sometimes I see the spirits of fish flying through the room here at night. I've asked Joey. He says they only appear every once in a while."

"Don't be crazy," she said and tried to look sternly at Anna. "Fish don't have spirits."

"Everything has a spirit," Anna smiled.

"You mean like the Egyptians believed?"

"I don't know," Anna shrugged. "Maybe you shouldn't believe everything I say."

"I don't," Emily grinned, "otherwise I wouldn't have been able to come here." She sat down on Anna's bed and crossed her legs. Her jeans were hanging loose on her. They were at least two sizes too big now, and she felt very satisfied with that. "My mom was very nervous about my coming here," she continued. "She thinks you're completely bananas!"

Anna laughed. "Your uncle told me. I know many people like your mother. When I was just a girl I worked for a woman who was like that. You know that when I was your age I had a baby. The woman I worked for refused to let me keep him with me. So my mother took care of him. He is big now. He lives in Johannesburg with his cousin. I hear from him sometimes. But I've lost him to the world."

Anna didn't seem sad. Emily wondered at her. "Do you miss him?" she asked.

"No." Anna shook her head. "I am always with him. My spirit is. He knows that."

"Do you really believe that everything has a spirit?" Emily asked, shifting on the bed.

"Yes," Anna said, and her eyes shone. "Of course. Everything. Even the mountain." Were her eyes twinkling,

Emily wondered, or was it just the reflection of the morning sunlight?

"But you I worry for. You are thin. Too thin," Anna remarked.

"Not thin enough," Emily replied firmly, and tapped her shoe on the floor. Anna sighed and tightened the scarf around her head. The roof was high and from its cobwebbed beams Emily could see insects twisting and dangling at the ends of fine, spidery threads.

"It's time for work," Anna said. "You can help me if you like."

Emily followed Anna out of the rondavel and they walked across the damp grass. The air was cool and the sun was just breaking through the mist. Haystacks were piled alongside a wooden fence. She could smell the horses. The paddock was made of dark wood and the stables had been repainted since Emily had last been there. Emily looked at the four horses standing at the far side of the paddock. The smell of mountain air was delicious, it was like eating something as you breathed. Emily played with a thread on her shirt and pulled it, unravelling the hem of her sleeve.

"Your uncle is next door in the stores, fixing the tractor," Anna said. "If you want him."

"No," Emily said. "I'll stay with you. Is that a new foal?"

"Born two weeks ago. Joey called him Brighton, after the town his mother came from."

"Whose mother?"

"Joey's mother, silly," Anna laughed. "She was English."

"Hmph." Emily shoved her hands into her pockets and walked up to the paddock. She wanted Anna to know that she wasn't interested in this "Joey" at all!

She stretched out her hand to the foal's brown muzzle and touched the small, damp nose. Then she rubbed the soft hair on the animal's neck. It shied away. "Pity horses don't stay this size," she said to Anna. "Then I wouldn't be the least bit scared of riding."

"Ah," Anna said. "That is something you still must learn."

Planting seedlings looked easy enough, but after two hours bent over, her hands rough from digging up the earth and her nails cracked and crusted with dirt, Emily was dizzy and her arms were weak. Her uncle cleared his throat and patted his stomach.

"Ready for lunch?" he asked.

Emily rocked back on her haunches and stuck out her legs, banging them to get the blood flowing again. The rows of planted seedlings stood to her left, and to her right was a wheelbarrow still full of little plants in black plastic packets.

"What am I actually planting?" Emily asked.

Uncle Tim laughed. "Ah. Some are vegetables and some are herbs. Certain herbs grow well with certain vegetables and keep bugs away from them. There's a whole art to it. Most people, including your mother, think I'm slightly bonkers, but I get wonderful results most years. I've learnt from our sangoma and from

Anna, for example, how one can plant tomatoes at a certain time, and if you take the moon's position into account, you can get really big tomatoes!"

"You believe in all that stuff?" Emily asked.

"You laughing at me?"

"Always," she said. "Haven't you figured me out by now?"

Uncle Tim laughed and changed the subject. "So, Em, are you still too poop-scared to ride horses?"

"I thought that was a dead subject."

"We'll have to get Joey to introduce you to the horses. Properly."

"What's all this stuff about Joey? Who's this Joey?" Emily eyed her uncle warily.

"There's no 'stuff about Joey,'" he said. "Joey lives on the farm. He talks to animals."

"This place is weird," Emily said.

"Not at all," said Uncle Tim. "He's very good. His father is a local Zulu man. His mother was, and I guess still is, English. She lives in England now."

The air was warm and Emily wiped sweat from her forehead. She took off her cap and eyed it with satisfaction. It had become suitably grubby. She looked up the landscaped hill to where Anna was gathering lavender at the top.

"Lunch time," Uncle Tim said. "Come and eat." He beckoned and turned, his sunburnt nose shiny-red. A traffic light. A stop sign. His nose was a stop sign. She was going mad. Anything, think of anything, just don't think of food. Not hungry — she was not hungry. Don't even think of the word. If she ate, say, just a handful of vegetables, then would that stretch her stomach?

By afternoon the sky was bright, clear blue. Emily stood in her room. She was full. All that food. List it:

1 large potato
1 (huge) slice of Anna's bread
2 spoons of gravy (no chicken)
1 cup of broccoli
1 cup of yoghurt (instead of ice cream) (less fat)
1 cup of tea with 1 spoon of sugar (16 calories per teaspoon, oh boy)
4 prunes (120 calories)
WORST OF ALL ... 20 almonds — 13g of FAT!!!!

december 19th
oh boy, oh boy. i have just made the biggest, fattest PIG of myself. emily you are a PIG and not even a flipping bathroom scale around this place to weigh yourself. it is now three pm i'm so tired i could just sleep, but sleeping stops your metabolism so in order to burn up all that i have disgustingly consumed today i will be staying up all night, try to run around and be active. climb the mountain or something. while we were planting anna said that on the farm next door terrible things happened and the farmer and his wife were murdered (and other horrible things) by their "servants," because for years the farm workers had been working almost like slaves ... revenge ... that's what anna said.

that's what a lot of all this violence is about, she said. then she said uncle Tim was a great man and EVERYONE *thought so i.e. he respects the land and asks traditional healers for advice and help etc. etc. and how he has helped so many people. anyway my mom called, a hasty hello-goodbye type of thing.*

Chapter 3

Emily stood in the steamy bathroom and wiped the mist from the mirror. She looked at her face and had to look again. Those funny shadows underneath her eyes were almost the same shape as on the face of the 5000-year-old man. Her chubby cheeks were gone, but the hips and legs ... still out of proportion to the rest. Maybe just lose two more kilos in that area. She heard crickets chirping loudly. The horses neighed from the paddock. Anna called them "Joey's horses." Joey.

One good thing was that her legs did not touch at the top any more. Her thighs were certainly thinning down. When she stood with her feet together there was a gap running all the way from her ankles to the top of her legs. Good job. Very good job.

Later in the evening, next to the crackling log fire in the lounge, Emily lay on her stomach and played with oil pastels on a piece of black paper. Uncle Tim leant back in his chair, reading the paper. His beard shone gold in the firelight, and although his eyes glittered and flamed, Emily could see only gentleness in his face. He wore the floppy sunhat at a rakish angle. He even wore that hat indoors. Even at night.

In the orange light of the burning logs, Emily used a white pastel and watched the colour change on the paper as the flames flickered up or died down. "Have you got any books on Egypt?" she asked, turning her head to face Uncle Tim.

"Egypt? Nope, I don't think so. Check the shelves."

Emily got up and her hand flew to her forehead. She sat down again abruptly. "Phew, sorry." She shook her head to clear away the spots that danced before her eyes.

Uncle Tim put down his paper. "Are you all right?"

"Of course," she said and smiled. The bookshelf against the wood-panelled wall was filled with agricultural books, books about farming and herbs, medicinal books. She opened a thick medical dictionary. There was the human body, a skeleton, filled in with veins and lungs and livers and brains and muscles in cross-section. Was all that stuff really inside her?

She took the book and placed it on the floor next to the piece of paper. First, in the black sky, she drew a large planet. It was egg-shaped and cracked in the centre. Out of the crack a skeletal figure emerged. The egg-planet was transparent and inside it the skeleton man was uncurling itself. Emily drew the bones, adding shadows where the fingers crept through the crack. Around the planet whirled fireballs and comets, and from the four corners of the page stretched the hooked fingers of acacia trees.

"You up to more planting tomorrow?" Uncle Tim asked.

"Sure," Emily said, without looking up.

"Anna tells me you're a slowcoach." She could hear the smile in his voice. "She says that you need a real introduction to farm life. You have some supper?"

"Yes ... thanks."

"What've you got down there?"

"Oh, nothing. Stupid drawing."

"Let me see ..." Uncle Tim rubbed his nose and leant forward. He was quiet. Emily did not look up from the paper.

"A skeleton?" he finally commented, his voice soft. "A skeleton emerging from an eggshell planet? Signifying ... uh, oh, let me think ... aha, that birth and death are the same in essence?"

"Very good," Emily said and laughed. "I'll take that explanation. Honestly, I haven't a clue what it *means!*"

"That reminds me," said Uncle Tim. "I don't mean to scare you, but please make sure that you don't wander off this property at any time, unless you are with Anna or someone from the farm. Don't go over the hill. I don't expect any trouble, but just be aware, Em, that where this territory ends, anything can happen. Okay?"

"I know," Emily said, looking into her uncle's kind eyes. "Anna told me what happened."

"Next door? Yes, that was awful ... but don't live in fear either. Around here, feel free. Talk to anyone, do whatever you like."

"Anna said that everyone around here thinks you're great."

Uncle Tim went slightly red.

"Do you speak Zulu, Uncle Tim?"

"Sure." He stood up and went out of the room. When he came back he was carrying a bowl of roasted nuts. "And you can learn too. Joey's half Zulu. You two can practise."

"Doesn't he speak English, though?" Emily asked.

"Oh yes," Uncle Tim said smiling. "Fluently." He took a handful of nuts and put them in his mouth. He leant over the old oak coffee table and Emily could hear him crunching, could smell the thick, hot aroma of almonds and cashews. No. She turned her head, blocked her nose from inside. Get back to the drawing. Think about the drawing. To the background of her sketch she added the high-rise buildings of Durban, smudged over with white smog.

"Aren't you having any?" Uncle Tim offered her the nuts.

"In a moment," she said, and bent her head over the paper. More details. More details in the skeleton. Define every finger bone, foot bone. What were they called? Metatarsals? Give them shadow, dimension. The more detail, the better.

"Uncle Tim, don't you ever get lonely?"

"Nope."

"Why not?"

"Because I'm such good company." He smiled.

"Aren't you ever going to get married?"

"Maybe. I'm still a spring chicken though. Thirty-four. And before you get married, you have to fall in love, you know."

"Oh!" Emily looked up at him slyly. "Are you in love?"

"Good grief!" he laughed out, colouring red. "Well, perhaps. But that's all I'm telling you at the moment. That's enough. What about you?"

"I have my drawing. I'll probably never get married.

No one ever likes me. I could never keep someone for more than a few hours. Anyone who really gets to know me won't be able to stand me after one day."

The logs spluttered and spark went up the chimney. The smell of pine filled the room. Jeepers, Emily thought. She had eaten more in one day than she'd eaten altogether in the entire previous week. Tomorrow she would starve.

i am writing in the dark, don't know what time it is. i have been dreaming of eating CAT FOOD ... *what's the matter with me? spent time with anna after supper and asked her more about spirits. she firmly holds to the egyptian theory (well, at least i think it's egyptian) that we all, including cats dogs horses etc, have spirits. also that there is* SOME-THING *out* THERE *watching and listening. oh boy! it gives me the creeps. so if* IT *is watching me, then i hope it enjoys the show. if i am just acting out my existence for some vast clever* BEING, *then i had better make it amusing at least, right? tomorrow am supposed to meet joey. what is so great about this joey? anna seems to speak about him as if he has something special that we do* NOT. *well, we'll see about that, ladies and frogs.*

The day began early again and Emily went to the bathroom. She washed her hair and as she ran her fingers over her scalp, soft, blonde wisps came away in her hand. She stared at her face and just for a moment struggled to recognize herself. She had blue-black rings under her eyes. Roosters crowed. The sun shone in dappled patches through the frosted glass of the bathroom window.

Anna was hanging her clothes on the washing line when Emily walked out of the house. Emily felt her skin hot and clammy beneath her long T-shirt and cut-off jeans. Her peaked cap was loose on her head.

Uncle Tim led the way to the stables with Emily trailing behind. Anna went straight up the hill to plant. In the distance smoke from the early-morning fires curled into the air and the horses in the paddock pawed the ground and snorted into the dawn. The green grass grew high above Emily's knees and left traces of dew along her calves. The stable doors were open.

"Joey!" Uncle Tim called in a loud, cheerful voice.

A dark-skinned boy with a thick mop of wavy black hair stood suddenly in the stable doorway. Emily's gaze locked with his. He was holding a metal bucket and his jeans were soaked from the knees down. He stepped out of the stables, walking jerkily, almost clumsily, reminding Emily somehow of a new-born foal. Emily stared at his jeans.

"This is my niece," Uncle Tim patted Emily's shoulder. "I thought it might be a good idea for her to help you muck out."

Joey looked her up and down. "Okay," he said. "It's pretty tough work though. Can you handle it?"

"'Course," Emily said. His eyes were a feline green, cool and clear. Emily glanced at his dark, cracked hands and wondered how old he was.

"So, it's stables instead of planting today," Uncle Tim said. "Enjoy yourselves." His voice seemed to blend in with the soft animal hums of the morning.

Emily stood with her arms folded loosely in front of her.

"What part of the job do you want to do?" Joey asked her, licking his plum-coloured lips as if he too were slightly nervous.

"Anything," Emily said. "I'll do anything."

Joey turned the hose on full and began to spray down the floors. Muck gathered in the corners and he indicated to Emily to fetch the broom and start sweeping the murky water towards the door.

After a while her arms and back ached. Joey didn't speak much. Eventually he turned and wiped his hair from his mud-streaked face.

"Wanna ride, later on?"

"I, uh, don't really ride," Emily replied nervously, leaning for a moment on the old broomstick.

"So?" Joey shook his head. "You can learn, can't you?"

Emily turned away and began to sweep furiously. She pulled her cap lower over her eyes. *I hate horses*, she wanted to say. But she didn't.

By midmorning they were finished and Emily helped Joey wash out the buckets and rinse out the broom. She peered up at him, and couldn't help staring for a moment at the light-green eyes which seemed strangely bright in his dark face. Her head spun. She didn't know how she would get out of riding unless she admitted how scared she was. And she wasn't about to do that. The dizziness continued. It had to be the result of overeating the day before. She tried not to think about lunch.

After the stables were clean, Emily went back to the house. Joey said he wouldn't be a minute. She hung around the house, watching the chickens, listening to the cattle lowing in the distance. Durban felt far away. She could smell food in the kitchen but dared not enter. Joey seemed to be taking his time. Half an hour later he came sauntering up to the farmhouse, swinging a saddle. Emily watched his strange, irregular walk. He stood at the steps of the veranda and squinted up at her. "You ready?" he said, and grinned.

Emily's horse looked far too large; she didn't like the size of the gap between the grassy meadow and the bottom of the horse's belly. She looked across the farm at the wide, blue mountains in the distance. The horses were a wonderfully chocolatey colour and Joey's had a blaze down the front of its nose. He saddled the horses and put reins and bits on both. He gave Emily a leg-up. She was surprised at his strength. The horse moved, stomped, snorted. Joey untethered it and held the reins. "Horses smell fear," he said. "So keep it to yourself."

Great, Emily thought. Now I have to be frightened about being frightened. "I trust you only because my uncle thinks you're okay," Emily narrowed her eyes.

"That's fine," Joey said. "I won't make the horse do anything you don't want it to do."

"Do you read minds, like your horses?" Emily asked.

He burst out laughing. "No," he shook his head. "We read feelings."

"Oh, I see," Emily said and looked fearfully at the ground.

Joey led the horses through the pastures and out along the farm road. The road wound through tall grass until eventually they reached a large cluster of trees. A breeze rustled the leaves and there was a strong smell of some potent plant.

"Eucalyptus," Joey said, and Emily looked at him out of the corner of her eye. Maybe she should have eaten, she thought. Just a tiny bit of something. She was feeling nauseous. She could hear rushing water and then the trees opened onto a clearing and the grass was luminous and lush and green. A small animal scuttled across the path and slipped into the grass before Emily could see exactly what it was. Joey stopped and threw Emily's reins to her.

"You can steer the rest of the way."

"But there isn't a brake pedal!"

"Pull in the reins," Joey said.

Branches scratched their skin as they ducked beneath the trees and rode onwards into the wood.

"Is this still the farm?" Emily asked.

"Oh yes, and it goes a lot further on to the west too." They rode for a while and then Joey turned and suddenly asked Emily: "Why do you have such dark rings under your eyes? Don't you sleep?"

Emily was stunned for a moment. How could he ask such a personal question? She lifted her nose and looked down at him. "No business of yours," she said.

"Sorry. Didn't mean to offend you. Hey, Em."

"Emily."

"Hey, Emily. It's just that if you're not in control the horses will feel it."

"I'm perfectly fine," Emily answered.

The trees grew closer together and Emily had to bend her head low. The rushing of the river grew louder and the smell of damp filled her nostrils. Moss-covered rocks appeared at intervals through the grass and suddenly she saw the lively, glinting gold of the river. The horse stopped as if familiar with the spot. Joey tethered his horse to a tree. Emily waited, trying to clear the fuzzy feeling from her head. A strange, floating sensation made her hold onto the mane tightly as Joey tethered her horse. He helped her down and she stood looking at the water. The wind blew up. Emily felt heavy. As she looked up, the sky above the green leaves began to whirl into a spiral. She blinked.

"Hey!" Joey called out, but his voice was far away. Then Emily sank down softly. It was a relief. The spinning ended. The grass felt soft and damp.

don't know what day it is
i have been in bed. anna's face was the first thing
i saw after fainting (i think) at the river. joey
brought me back to the house, and the horse with
him. anyway, uncle Tim and anna are convinced i
am SICK *(in the mind) ha ha, and so have*
sentenced me to bed. good job anyway since i am
too pathetically weak to get up. i think i will be
the author of a book ... lazy person's guide to farm
work. i feel sort of ashamed that i passed out like
that. now joey will really have a bad view of me.

Uncle Tim stood over Emily's bed in the flickering candlelight. She could see the way his beard curled out, sort of like a beak. He was a giant, his shadow on the wall huge and round, and Emily rubbed her eyes to see that he was holding out a cup of something steaming and hot.

"Soup," he said firmly. "Drink it."

Emily turned her head away and complained.

"Come on," he said. "This is serious. Don't you realize what's going on, Emily?"

"I do," she heard herself moan. "I'm silly. I'm making a fool of myself, that's what. I can't even take a tiny bit of exercise. Toughen me up, Anna says. I need more training to do farm work, you're right."

"Sshh," her uncle said. Emily feared he had lost his sense of humour.

"Okay, okay, I'll drink," she said apologetically.

He placed the cup next to the bed on a small wooden box that served as a bedside table. Emily sniffed and smelt the faint aroma of herbs. Herbs and vegetables. Her stomach had tied itself into a tight knot. She lifted her head and looked at the cup. Carrots swam together with celery sticks. The vegetables seemed to swell and grow huge, and she blinked. They were alive, and wanted to force their way into her mouth. They were out to get her. Stay away from them, she warned herself. It's a plot. You'll be deceived into eating them and then you'll be sorry. She clenched her teeth.

"Oh," she sighed and lay back against the pillow. "I just *can't*. Don't you see, Uncle Tim? It's totally impossible!"

"What are you talking about, Em?"

"I just can *not* eat anything. I mean, even if I want to, I can't." She spoke quietly and managed to grin half-heartedly.

Uncle Tim took a deep breath and put his hands into his pockets. He paced up and down the floor. Then he turned around and rubbed his eyes. "Goodnight, Em," he said. "I hope you'll try to drink some of that. Even just a sip." His eyes looked tired and he put his hand on his big, floppy sunhat.

"Uncle Tim?"

"Yip?"

"Afraid of sunburn?"

"Definitely," he smiled. He left the room and Emily saw Anna's shadow in the doorway. Uncle Tim stopped. She heard them talking in low tones. Then she thought she saw her uncle place his arm for a second on Anna's shoulder.

i am writing by candlelight again. okay, so today is december 21st and christmas is around the corner. my mom wanted to come here for christmas, she said, but then something came up with warren so she'll be with him instead, which is a relief. i can't keep food down, even if i want to. i know this is serious, but what can i do? besides, i am now almost the size i want to be. if i eat ANYTHING, i know i am sure to grow ENORMOUS. i am sorry that i passed out on joey only hours after we'd met. i hope to see him tomorrow. i'm still just as scared of horses, though, as i ever was.

wimp. anna said goodnight to me a minute ago.
she has some idea that i should go with her to
visit the sangoma on the hill, very soon. she
utterly believes all that stuff ... i am so tired i can
hardly hold the pen straight. once more there
have been a few violent incidents not far from
here. goodnight until ...

Joey walked slowly towards the rondavel so that Emily could keep up with him. She was still feeling shaky and her knees quivered slightly as she stepped through the grass. The sun warmed her arms and she noticed only then how pale her skin had become.

Joey opened the door to the room adjoining Anna's.

"Welcome to my home," he grinned. Emily peeped through before she stepped inside. It was a strange room. Very bare. A bedside table and a mattress on the floor. A grass mat and a tape recorder. A few books and some small sculptures carved out of soapstone.

"I have a friend who brings me the stones," Joey said. "Come in."

"You *make* these?" Emily looked at the figures that stood against the straight wall that divided the rondavel into two.

"Course," Joey waved his hand. "So? What do you think?" He sat down on his mattress and looked at her.

"Well, it's nice, but ..." Emily shrugged her shoulders and rolled her eyes across his bare walls and floor. "It's so empty."

"I like it this way," Joey said. "I find cluttered places suffocating."

"How did you come to live here?" Emily asked, walking around the room, inspecting it, trying to find out what kind of person Joey was. The room itself revealed very little. It was the kind of room that her mother would abhor. There were spiders basking in the sunlight on the windowsill.

"I ran away from school," Joey said. "My father is very traditional. He lives in the village and I couldn't really go to him. He would have been terribly embarrassed. One of the village women knew Anna, and said I should find her and speak to her. So I did. She told me about your uncle and I came to him and we became friends. He's the kindest man I know."

"Why did you leave school?" She was standing a few metres from Joey. His hands were linked around his knees, and he looked up at her through thick, dark eyelashes.

"I hated it," he said, and his mouth twisted.

"Why?"

"Why?" he laughed almost bitterly. "Because I was an outsider."

"An outsider?" Emily persisted stupidly. Joey sighed and shook his head. Then he got up.

"Forget it," he said stiffly. "Let's talk about something else."

Emily had been on the brink of asking him all about himself, about his family. Now she was even more curious, but she knew that she was treading on dangerous ground.

"Okay," she said.

"So now you've seen my house," Joey said abruptly.

"We might as well go and brush the horses."

"Might as well," Emily replied, and they walked out of the rondavel.

For a while, as they made their way to the paddock, there was nothing to say. Then Joey stopped suddenly and turned to her.

"I've told you my story. Now you tell me what sickness you've got."

"What?" Emily put her hands on her hips and looked him straight in the eye. "What are you talking about? I'm perfectly fine."

"You're lying," Joey responded roughly, and turned his head away from Emily and began to walk quickly to the horses.

Chapter 4

It began to rain in the early hours of the morning. Emily looked out of foggy windows to see the mist creeping low over the grass. Her neck ached. She felt her ribs against the bedding and put her hands to her face, rubbing her cheeks.

"Emily!" Anna's urgent whisper came from the doorway. "You awake?"

"Yes, what?"

"Come and see," Anna said. Emily jumped out of bed. Black and red spots flashed in front of her eyes. She pulled on a pair of jeans and followed Anna outside. Her feet were cold and her long nightshirt ballooned around her like a tent. It was still drizzling. The air was cool and leaves dripped noisily onto the muddy edges of the veranda steps. Emily could hear Uncle Tim's voice through the fine mist, and she could hear his boots squelching in the mud. Anna stopped on the bottom step.

"Oh, Emily," she said. "Please fetch some towels. And a blanket." Then she hurried into the mist.

Emily ran back inside, feeling confused. What was going on? She went into the bathroom, pulled two large towels off the rack and then took the blanket off her bed. She ran back outside. Somewhere in the distance Anna was talking rapidly in Zulu. A baby cried.

After a moment or so Anna rushed back up to the veranda. In her arms she held a small bundle. Emily looked closer and saw that the bundle moved. A tiny leg kicked and Emily saw with a start that Anna was carrying a baby. Emily held out the towels. Uncle Tim came briskly up to the veranda through the mist, a number of farm workers behind him. Lastly came Joey, brushing past her, out of breath. Everyone was talking loudly in Zulu and Emily didn't understand a word. Why wouldn't anyone tell her what was going on? Anna wrapped one of the towels around the baby, who cried helplessly, sadly. Its voice was so weak it was barely there. Anna went inside and Emily was left staring at her uncle. He shook his head and sprayed her with droplets of rain.

"Well, well," he said. "I think we should all have some tea!"

In the kitchen Emily watched Joey fill the huge kettle. When he was finished she went to stand at his side. "Mind telling me what's going on?" she asked. "What happened? What's that baby doing here?"

"I found him. Somebody dumped him on a haystack in the field. I heard him crying for hours before I got up and went to see what was happening. I couldn't believe what I was seeing."

"Jeez, you mean somebody just left him out there, to ... to ..."

"Yes," Joey said. He flicked his hair out of his eyes. His clothes were soaking wet. "I'm freezing. I hope the baby won't die. Anna's got him now, so he should get well."

"Is he sick?"

"Didn't you see how small he is? He's sick, all right."

The kitchen was hot and crowded with people and the windows were misting up from the inside. The workers' big boots were all lined up at the kitchen door. Joey made tea for everyone.

"Wanna sit in the lounge?" Joey carried through two steaming cups. Emily walked carefully, listening. It sounded as though Anna was in the next room with the baby. Her bedroom. She felt drawn towards it.

"Don't." Joey looked at Emily and his green eyes flashed. "Leave her with him for now. She'll call you if she wants you. Or she'll come out when she's ready."

In the lounge, Emily sat on the edge of her chair. She fidgeted with her hair, trying to pull her fringe low over her nose.

"Why are you pretending that you're fine?" Joey asked. "I can see you aren't. Why can't you just tell me what's wrong with you? You can tell me, you know ..."

"No. You don't understand. I'm not really sick, Joey. Okay? Let's just say I made myself like this, okay?"

"You're starving yourself to death, aren't you?" Joey looked at her and she saw an angry light in his green eyes. "You're like those kids in magazines. City kids. Making themselves sick. For nothing. Anorexia, that's what they call it. It's in your eyes. You should go to the sangoma."

"Thanks for your advice," Emily said drily and got up, clenching her fists as she walked towards the door. "Next time I'll remember to ask you for it."

"Don't," Joey got up. "I didn't mean to upset you. Anna told me that ..."

"She had no business telling *you* anything about *me*, okay!" Emily shouted.

"Wait," Joey said. "Don't be angry. I'll tell you something, okay? Something about me that no one knows."

Emily stopped on her way to the door. She turned around and saw Joey holding out one of the cups of tea. She looked at his strangely rough hands. They seemed old and worn even though Joey himself was young.

"Don't look away and pretend you didn't see," Joey said softly. "Yes, I've got hands that look prehistoric. When I was little they used to call me Wrinkle-Skin. Here, have some tea."

Emily reached out and took the handle of the cup. She took a sniff of the tea. It would go down into her stomach and stretch it. No, thank you. She put the cup down again. The baby began to cry loudly from her room.

"I want to see what's going on," Emily said, walking across the room. She stubbed her toe against the door and hopped noisily over the floor to her bedroom.

The baby lay on her bed, wrapped tightly in a red-and-yellow bath towel. Anna bent over him and dabbed his tiny face with baby oil. She had just given him a bath, and the tub of warm water still lay on the floor at the foot of Emily's bed.

"Can I help?" asked Emily quietly.

"No, it's all right now," Anna said. "Come and look."

Emily took a step closer. She had never seen such a tiny baby. His whole head was hardly bigger than an orange. His eyes were closed. He had a low, sad cry, which sounded as though he had given up, as though he didn't expect to be held when Anna picked him up to comfort him. Emily swallowed. His hand pushed out from the towel and she couldn't believe how tiny it was, how small the fingers were. His neck was terribly thin.

"How old do you think he is?" Emily asked Anna.

"Two weeks, maybe." Anna said. She patted his back and rocked him. "He's very small. I've seen it before — babies left to die. Sometimes they die anyway, even if they are fed. Of broken hearts. We'll call him Sipho." Anna looked at Emily and the hint of a smile tugged at the corner of her mouth.

afternoon
definition by joey, the walking english-zulu
dictionary. sipho=gift. often a name given to a
child very much wanted by its parents. ha ha.
(but not really a joke). he was abandoned and so
now WE HAVE a baby! his head, tho' tiny, is too big
for his body. he looks all out of proportion. it's so
sad. this morning i have eaten NOTHING. i am
feeling dizzy, but will not, for the life of me, go
and get FOOD. this whole thing has gone a bit too
far. i just pulled out two CHUNKS of my hair an
hour ago. CHUNKS i say. i really got a fright. this i
can hardly write, so get it over with because it
has to be admitted. i haven't had
myperiodforalongtime.

uncle Tim is going to durban overnight and
will see my mom. hate to admit i have hardly
given her a thought lately, but i'm sure she's fine
with whatsisface. so i don't quite know why this

*sudden venture off to durban, but i'm glad i'm
here on the farm. i hoped he wasn't going to ask
me if i wanted to go back, or anything. and he
didn't, dear uncle T. i promise now that i am
going to learn to make a horse stop and go,
without dying of fright.*

Emily went out into a gleaming morning, rushing
through the jewels of water clinging to the grass. Joey
was waiting for her at the stables. He had already
saddled up and was picking a stone from his horse's
hoof.

"I half expected you to chicken out," Joey said.

"Never," Emily answered.

"There was an attack on one of the nearby villages
last night," Joey said, still examining the hoof.

The air was thick with moisture. Green fields waved
in the light breeze and droplets clung to the fine mate-
rial of Emily's socks. Her legs began to tremble.

"Why?" she whispered.

"I dunno." Joey didn't look up at her. "A revenge
thing, maybe. Senseless unless you know millions of
details. Maybe senseless even then. Four people
killed."

"Will they come here?" Emily's voice was still, her
throat was tight.

"I don't think so. Your uncle has worked very hard to
keep out of it all. He is sometimes asked to keep
weapons, or to inform people about other people, but
he never does it. And they sort of respect him. All of
them. And then there's the sangoma."

"What's he got to do with it?" Emily let out a long breath.

Finally Joey looked at her. He let go of the horse's hoof. "Let me give you a leg-up. I'll tell you while we ride."

The mud sprayed up under them as they began to trot up the farm road that wound its way to the foot of the mountain. The sun shone down on the glistening trees and wherever Emily looked she saw pearls and starbursts of light. Her legs were feeling almost numb. She could look down at her toes as she bounced uncomfortably along, jolting up and down on the saddle, and command them to wiggle. They would obey, but they felt disconnected. Horses smell fear, but surely not the kind of fear she was feeling now?

The road narrowed until it became a pathway. They slowed the horses to a walk, finding their way between the boulders and rocks that marked the way up the hill.

"You'll rattle your teeth out if you ride like that," Joey said over his shoulder. "To trot you have to work hard, move up on every second beat, not just bounce along like a floppy rag doll. Find the rhythm or lose your teeth. That's the long and short of it."

"Tell me about the witch doctor."

"Sangoma."

"Whatever."

"Ride up alongside me." Joey stretched out his hand and Emily's horse moved towards him, touching his hand with its muzzle. Emily wondered at Joey's command of her horse.

"The sangoma is deeply respected by all people. He is the real authority around here, but not officially.

He's foretold the future and has never been wrong. He won't do that often. He has a strange power, which the people say he harnesses from the mountains. And he uses that to heal people. At the same time everyone is kind of afraid of him. You see, he also has the power to place curses."

"What on earth does this have to do with my uncle?" Emily wiped a small river of sweat from her forehead.

"Well, if the sangoma recognizes that a person has a gift or power and chooses to protect that person, then no one on earth can harm that person."

"Oh, come on, Joey ..."

Joey laughed and shrugged and shook his head. Then he pushed his horse on in front of Emily and they ascended the mountain.

The grass grew drier and the path less muddy. Soon they reached an embankment which allowed them to stop and look around. The view stretched out before them, a patchwork of rolling hills, spreading outwards to steep and shadowed mountains. Joey pointed to the mountain directly opposite.

"There. Up in a cave. That's where the sangoma lives. It's only a two-hour climb to get to him."

"So?" Emily looked at him and reined in her horse as it attempted to wander.

"Anna told me she thinks you should go ..."

"Listen, Joey," Emily butted in, feeling her cheeks grow hot. "Just how much do you know about me? I didn't give Anna permission to discuss me with *you*!" The horse flicked its mane and pawed the ground.

"Sshh," Joey said, and put his finger over his lips. The horse shivered and shrugged and immediately became still. Joey turned to Emily again. "Anna has almost adopted me, since I arrived. She told me I could trust her, and she told me to be open with her. We talk about everything. She has a lot of faith in our generation, Emily, so we talk about *everything*. But if you don't want us to talk about you, then we won't. That's only fair."

Emily sat on her horse in sullen silence. The wind blew through her hair and she felt it right on her scalp, which reminded her how thin her hair had become. She flicked the fringe from her eyes and then she shrugged.

"No, it's okay," she said, more to the ground than to Joey. "I mean, you can talk about whatever you want to talk about."

well, it's rather strange. uncle T returned from durban and brought news of my mom ... apparently not well. he arrived back last night and didn't look good, i have to say. i don't get it. what is actually WRONG with my mother? is she having a nervous BREAKDOWN? how do you know what that is anyway? he said she's on medication because she can't cope. with what? there have been incidents of violence quite near here, but apparently uncle Tim is under the good spell of a WITCH DOCTOR and so nothing can harm him. oh, and news is that my mom and her present, uh, FRIEND (surfer) have split. this is most likely to

have been the cause for her breakdown, who
knows. the show goes on. i can sort of ride a horse
(good) and i have not eaten much today (very
good). i've been helping anna take care of sipho.
he looks so small, and only half alive. sometimes
he has tears coming out of his eyes and doesn't
make a sound. i wonder if anna is right about
babies dying of broken hearts. imagine leaving
someone to die! thassall. i can't write about joey.

Wind rattled through the wooden window frames of the farmhouse in the late afternoon. Uncle Tim sat making new beehives and Emily sat in the lounge staring into the space between the cracks above the fireplace. She flicked the crumpled end of the drawing that she had shoved carelessly between two large books. She, Emily, careless with her drawings! It was true. She had stopped caring, she realized, about anything. She didn't even care if she didn't get up in the morning. This way, it was nice. She didn't have to be afraid of anything. Not of horses, not of the violence on the neighbouring farms. So it didn't even matter to her that she could now canter and gallop, and that it was Christmas Eve and she was sitting exactly where she had hoped to be when she was in Durban imagining her holidays. A branch hung over the fireplace, covered with gold-painted pinecones. There were no gifts. Only cards. Homemade biscuits and chocolates hung from strings on the branches. Anna had made them all.

"Uncle Tim, how was my mom?" Emily asked cautiously.

"Well," he mused. "She wasn't too bad."

"Is she angry with me?" Emily asked. Uncle Tim turned.

"You? No, of course not."

"I think she is. It's my fault. She blames me for her state."

"Don't be ridiculous, Em. If she blames anyone, she blames herself."

"Listen, we both know that my mother doesn't blame herself for anything." Emily stared dully at her uncle.

"She feels responsible, Em. She thinks you're starving yourself because she hasn't given you enough attention."

Emily stood up and ran her hand through her hair. The wind whipped against the glass and light dappled the lounge floor. Leaves and branches in movement. Shadows. All over the floor Emily saw shadows. Her own was long and thin, and bent at the knees as it went up the wall on the other side of the room.

"So you went to Durban because of me?" Emily said quietly. A few strands of her hair had come away between her fingers.

"Yip."

"But why?"

"Actually because your mom was insisting that you come back. I told her that if you can't recover here, you're not likely to recover anywhere. I took full responsibility for you. Now you have to help me." He looked at her intently, and Emily bit the inside of her cheek.

"Jeepers, Uncle T, you make it sound so *serious!*" she said.

"It *is* serious! You have got to start doing something to get better. You've become a grey shadow. I can hardly recognize you. You're walking like an old woman. I'll lighten up when I see you returning to yourself, Em, now come on!"

christmas eve
everyone gathered around the old branch and
sang silent night. well it wasn't a silent night
cos the wind was howling around the place ...
and nkosi sikelel' i'afrika ... and sipho was
there, still crying his sad low cry. the others
killed a goat. (uncle T says that's the tradition,
and even he ate the meat, YUK) i nearly hurled
my gut just thinking about it. anyway and then
we all had tea and cake and cookies, (i watched)
joey was only there for a short while, then went
off. we didn't say anything to each other. he
looked at me once. i couldn't understand, they
all spoke in zulu. anyhow, everyone has just
gone to bed and i crept back into the lounge,
found what was left of the cake and finished it.
and hate myself for it. you pig. disgusting fat
pig. i feel sick. and my mom has lost her
marbles. oh what a pretty mess this all is, ladies
and pigs, i tell you!

Emily stood silently at the foot of Anna's bed in the rondavel. Evening light cast a pink glow on the white walls. Sipho squirmed in a bundle of blankets and Anna gave Emily a helpless look as she placed a glass bottle next to her bed. The teat of the bottle looked far too large for the baby's tiny mouth.

"Goat's milk," Anna said and pursed her lips. "It is the closest to mother's milk. And he won't take it."

Emily sat down on Anna's bed and touched Sipho's cheek. It felt too soft to be skin. His hands moved erratically. His eyes would sometimes open halfway, as if he was afraid to see where he was.

"I want him to get well," Anna said to Emily. "Babies need food, but they also need love. I already love him as if he were my own. He must get well. Here, you try to feed him."

Anna lifted him, careful to keep her large hand behind his head. He was so weak he couldn't keep his head from flopping back violently. Emily was afraid that he might break as Anna placed him in her arms. She took the bottle, and had to smile. It was an old, glass Coke bottle, tightly fitted with a teat. She recognized it as a construction of Uncle Tim's. He had often used such bottles to feed motherless baby lambs. Emily held the bottle to Sipho's lips.

Outside, the sky grew dark. Crickets chirruped insistently and Emily's legs felt cold. Sipho's head rested on her arm. Soon the shadow of the sangoma's mountain fell over Anna's room and she walked across the floor and lit a candle.

"You know," she said to Emily, "I still prefer candlelight to electricity. In my village, when I was a child, they used to say I was mad because I liked to

63

sleep outside, to wake up to the song of the birds and the dew on my face. And even when I was older and we had electricity, I still used my candle for light."

Anna's shadow flickered to life on the floor. In the yellowness of the candlelight Emily thought she saw, flickering across Sipho's little sleeping face, the face of the 5000-year-old man. He seemed aged and wrinkled beyond all recognition. And then she saw that the baby's small, curled-up body was the same as that of the ancient man. Sipho was so young that he could have been old, so barely alive that he was almost dead. He could have died and stayed this tiny for thousands of years.

"The sangoma wants to see you," Anna said suddenly. She smiled. Her slanted eyes were so dark that Emily couldn't distinguish the iris from the pupil. "Don't worry. I have told him about you."

"You seem to tell a lot of people about me," Emily said.

"Yes, I do!" Anna's eyebrows went up and Emily caught the laughter in her eyes.

"Listen, Anna, maybe you believe in all that stuff, and everyone else around here might believe it too, but I'm strictly a here-and-now type. I believe in what I see."

"Like your mother?" Anna added, taunting her.

"No!" Emily exclaimed, wondering how Anna knew so much about her mother. She remembered how Uncle Tim's arm had touched Anna's shoulder that evening outside her room. "No, not like my mother at all. I don't mean to put down your beliefs — or Joey's or Uncle Tim's — but this sangoma stuff is a bit creepy to me, okay?"

Anna laughed out loud and Sipho woke up. Emily realized that her arm was tingling from holding it in one position for so long, and that she was seeing black-and-white flashes in front of her eyes. Don't eat, whatever you do, just don't eat, she warned herself. You've been enough of a pig already.

"I'm glad," said Anna, "that you don't just believe what people tell you. I'm like that too. But I think you should come with me to the sangoma to see for yourself. Here, give Sipho to me. I'll see you back at the house later."

Emily stumbled through the dark. Her feet hurt on the cold stones. Her stomach ached and churned and groaned. "Oh, be quiet, will you?" she mumbled into the night, pushing herself to hurry through the long grass. She made as much noise as she could to frighten away any snakes or sangomas that might possibly be lying in wait.

Chapter 5

december 27th

good evening ladies and gentlemen, i am writing from a position of luxury having fallen again in the presence of poor joey. i blacked out but at least this time with a whole display of stars, planets and other celestial floaties (the show was grand). i am now in bed and a raving mad uncle is trying to feed me with a teaspoon every half hour. he has some herbal mixture which smells like it could kill me. perhaps he is taking this thing more seriously than even i am. (yes i know it's bad and i need help etc. etc.) i overheard uncle T on the phone, he was obviously talking to my mom. he said, in a very un-Tim-like voice: meryl, all she needs is a lifetime of fresh air and tranquility. (that's me!) so now, from us in the studio, goodnight (or maybe morning).

Emily walked unsteadily through the bush towards the vegetable garden at the end of the paddock. She carried a basket and found the ripe tomato plants tangling all over the ground, red tomatoes peering out of green leaves, large and heavy and swollen. The whole plant was full of huge red tomatoes.

Emily put her hair behind her ears and bent down with her basket. She took a tomato and rubbed it between her hands, feeling the soft, shiny skin. Then she bit into it. The juice spilt over her lips and she caught it with her finger. The taste was heavenly. Tomatoes did not have that many calories, she thought. You could eat quite a lot of them and not put on weight. If you lived off cucumbers and lettuce and tomatoes, you would never get fat. But then perhaps it would make you want to start eating other things, like fruit and bread, and then of course it would start all over again. Emily had no idea how much she weighed, but she knew by the way her clothes were hanging on her that she was thinner than when she'd arrived on the farm. She had controlled herself well, but it was out of hand now, her control.

Uncle Tim had stood over her bed the evening before and said: "Em, if you carry on like this, you'll die."

Emily put the basket down. She finished eating the tomato and looked in the direction of Anna's bungalow. Sipho's cry echoed across the farm. A little while later she spotted Anna coming from the rondavel with Sipho tied tightly to her back. Emily wiped her hands on her jeans. She walked across the vegetable garden and met Anna at the fence.

"Hello," Anna said. "What are you doing?"

"Eating."

"Is that so?"

"Uncle Tim says I should eat only raw things that come from the farm. He says that none of it will make me fat."

"I see," Anna nodded. She hummed as she rocked Sipho.

"I've been thinking," Emily began. "About the sangoma. Do you think he could help? I mean, do you think he would be able to get me to eat ... without me getting fat?"

"Hmm," Anna rubbed her nose thoughtfully. She straightened the cloth she wore around her head. "I don't know. You want to visit him?"

"I'm not really sure."

"I think you do."

"Is he ... scary?"

"Oh no! Well, maybe for white people. The only white person who has been to him is your uncle. But I'll go with you."

Emily watched Anna's retreating back. Sipho was just a bump, a small protrusion. Emily thought how she would like to draw that, how his body fitted so snugly onto Anna's back. Emily bent down over the tomato plants again and filled her basket. This would be her food for the day, she thought. Each day now, she would choose one fruit or vegetable, and eat only that. If you ate only one type of food that made it easier for your digestion. That way you would be less likely to put on weight.

Uncle Tim was putting the finishing touches on his beehives and was outside the farmhouse when Emily arrived swinging her basket.

"Looks like you've got quite a lot there," he said and smiled.

"Tons. Monsters. Look at the size of this one!"

"So, have you had a good day?" Uncle Tim asked. "You know it was Anna who suggested that you do this."

69

"Really? I thought it was one of your bright ideas." She went and sat down on the veranda steps. She crossed her legs and leant back, shading her eyes from the sunlight. "Listen, Uncle Tim," she said, "I don't know how all these things are supposed to help me, because I can't argue with myself, you know. My mind's made a decision, and there's not much I can do about it. It's out of my hands."

He finished sanding one of the beehive doors. The edges were smooth. Sweat dripped from his bushy eyebrows into his eyes and he flicked his head, blinking.

"I thought I'd go with Anna to the sangoma," Emily said.

"Really?" He looked at her. "When?"

"Don't know yet. Sometime. And another thing: Have you seen Joey anywhere?"

"In the stores. Fixing a saddle."

Emily ambled along the stony road that led to the stores. She kicked the dust with her foot and wiped her arm across her face. She passed by the dam and heard the water splashing from the pipe. She could not see above the huge, grey wall of the dam. On the side of the wall, surrounded by thick trees, a metal ladder led over and into the water. Emily turned off the path and walked towards it. Reaching the ladder through the bush, she began to climb until she could see into the dam. The water was brown but not murky, and she could see right to the bottom. The sun played on the surface of the water and turned it to gold and silver. Emily dipped in her hand and brought some of it to her lips. It tasted sweet. So sweet that she had to have more. She splashed her face and then, looking to make sure that no one was around, she pulled off her jeans. Holding her nose, she jumped from the ladder into the water. Her shirt and pants clung to her as she sank beneath the surface. She saw gold ripples and thousands of bubbles and she swam to the other side. Swimming was the best exercise. You could burn up hundreds of calories. The only problem was that she didn't have that much energy. If she ate little and swam lots, she would not get fat.

"Hey, who's there?"

Emily spun around at the sound of Joey's voice. Her heart raced unreasonably. She swam to the side and pressed her body against the wall. She peered over the edge. Joey emerged from the trees. He looked up at her and his eyes were huge. His hair was matted and tangled and full of leaves. He seemed startled and flustered.

"I'm sorry," Joey stuttered and stepped back through the trees. "I ... didn't know it was you."

A second later he had vanished through the bush. She heard the door to the stores creak open and slam shut.

Emily let herself back into the water. She could see Joey's dark face in her mind. He had an interesting face.

She surfaced and shook her head, spraying droplets out all over across the surface of the water. Waves slopped up against the side of the wall. Eventually she grew tired of swimming and made her way to the ladder, pulling herself weakly from the water. Waves lapped against the sides of the dam wall long after she had pulled her jeans over her wet underwear and scrambled onto a hot granite rock to dry her shirt in the sun.

Some time later Joey came walking cautiously through the trees.

"Joey?" Emily called.

"You called me?"

"Yes. I'm here on the rock. Why don't you come up here?" Emily looked down at her shirt. It was almost dry. Her hair was plastered down onto her scalp.

Joey pushed branches aside and walked towards her. He seemed more awkward than usual. He was chewing on a long stalk of grass. Every now and again he spat a bit of it aside. He rubbed his nose and came to sit at the foot of the slanted rock.

"You okay?" he asked.

"Fine, I s'pose," Emily said. Then she looked him squarely in the eye. "Why did you say you were an outsider the other day, and then not say any more?"

Joey shrugged. Then he spoke. "After I was born my mother left me at my father's doorstep. She was an English lady who had come out to Africa, and she thought that by having an affair with a black person, she could somehow be a part of Africa. That's what I've put together from what my father tells me about her. And then me! She didn't want that! She went back to England and left money for my education in a special fund. So I went to Hilton, a colonial, mainly white private school. I hated it. I left as soon as I turned sixteen. I had no friends there. Nobody wanted to know me. The black kids were in one group, the whites in another. And I floated in between. And of course I had these dry, wrinkled hands — my mark of alien ... hood!" He smiled. "Jeez, I can't believe I'm saying this to you. And I want to say, I s'pose, that I can't understand why you're doing this to yourself."

"Is that why you talk to horses?" Emily asked suddenly, ignoring what he'd said about her.

"Who told you that?"

"Anna."

"Listen, I know you think I'm freaky, but let me tell you ..."

"No, you don't understand," Emily said. "I don't think you're freaky at all. At least ... not any more. You aren't any stranger than I am, anyway. And me? Why do I do this? 'Cos I want to be normal!"

december 28th
joey has gone for a day or so to visit his father. he used to spend his holidays in the rural village and then go back to school. i'm going tomorrow with anna to see the witch doctor. and i'm not doing this because i believe there is anything he can do. okay? (me) ... this is mainly out of curiosity.

Emily was up just before dawn and went silently to the rondavel. Early clouds scudded across the lightening horizon and the sky changed from deep indigo to light pink. Ducks quacked and the valley dogs barked. Emily held her shirt tightly to her and rubbed the goosebumps which appeared on her arms. She knocked on Anna's door. Anna let her in.

"What will you do with him?" Emily whispered,

peering past Anna's head at the small bundle on her bed.

"Take him with us. On my back."

"Isn't it far?"

"Two hours. I am used to this. Don't worry."

Anna's face was shiny and awake. She rubbed cream into her cheeks and offered some to Emily.

"No thanks. Look. Spots."

"That's from not eating," Anna remarked, without really looking.

Not eating? It was not quite true. That morning Emily had eaten a leftover baked potato which had been put in foil and left in the fridge. She felt sick just thinking about it, full and bloated, as if she would explode.

With Sipho tied tightly to her back, Anna left the rondavel and closed the door. Emily followed her through the grass as they headed west towards the mountains.

The sun rose and turned the green, waving grass to orange and yellow. A dam in the far distance shone gold and the mountains rapidly changed colour from pink to purple to green. Already it was warm and Emily could feel the heat of the sun on her shoulders. Sipho slept. They didn't speak. Eventually they reached the western border of the farm and turned north. The path disappeared into grass, and Emily put one foot after the other in Anna's footsteps. Soon the path became rocky and they reached the foot of the mountain. Emily looked up. Granite boulders towered over her. Lichen and moss grew on the rocks. Some of the boulders jutted out in strange and precarious angles, as though they might topple and roll at any moment.

"This is where the Spirit of the Mountain lives," Anna said, turning. Her face dripped with perspiration. She blinked rapidly. Emily looked at the sleeping child on Anna's back. She wanted to offer to carry him for a while, but she knew her legs would collapse. Her head swam and white flecks appeared just in front of her eyes, swimming here and there, wherever she looked. What was Anna talking about?

"Are you trying to say ... really and truly ... that a *spirit* lives here?"

Anna smiled. "Nervous? Follow me."

The path became increasingly difficult to climb. Sometimes Emily had to grasp rocks with both hands to keep herself from falling backwards. Anna kept a steady pace, climbing higher and higher until they reached a point where the steep cliff above them blocked out the light of the sun. There, Anna took a deep breath.

"Now you go in front," she said. A lizard scuttled over the sand in front of them and vanished under a rock.

"What?"

"Turn left there, then follow the crevice. That is the custom. The person he sees first is the one. He must not see me first."

"Wait. Hang on a moment, Anna! Okay, listen ... just tell me ... give me some idea what he looks like."

Anna wiped her forehead again. She smiled and

made her eyes huge, resembling an owl. She stuck out her tongue and pulled a face, waving her hand crazily behind her head.

"Great," Emily huffed, and turned away, looking up.

Somewhere she could hear water dripping. There was a hollow echo after each splash and Emily followed the curve of the rock, walking on the small path that now appeared, worn and sandy beneath her feet. Anna kept some distance behind, Sipho's small cry resounding off the rocks. Suddenly Emily rounded a bend and found herself facing a huge overhang. The rock formed a massive, flat ceiling that seemed to retreat right into the mountainside.

Water gushed from a stream above the overhang, falling into a pothole the size of a bathtub. The falling water formed a thin curtain across the entrance to a cave. Emily stopped and swallowed. Then she stepped through.

There was a movement at the far side of the cave. A smell of mould and damp wafted towards her and she licked her lips nervously. It smelt ancient, prehistoric. The whole place could have been something out of the Stone Age. She looked back. Anna was behind her. She waved Emily on, encouraging her to go deeper into the cave. Emily took one shaky step forward. This was what she imagined it might feel like inside a pyramid. She took a closer look at the farthest corner of the cave.

An old car windscreen stood between her and him. Behind the glass Emily could see a multitude of strange objects scattered on the cave floor: a doll's arm, chicken bones, cow bones, a plastic ring, stones, shells and beads lay spread out in front of him. He himself crouched on his haunches, his hands clasped together. His eyes stared at her intently. A leather thong threaded with lion's teeth hung around his neck. His chest was bare and he was wearing blue jeans.

Emily stared at him. Was this it? This was the *sangoma*? A guy in jeans with a heap of junk behind an old windscreen in a cave? Ha!

"Come!"

The voice echoed through the cave and repeated itself. Emily took another step forward and looked at the old chicken bones lying at the sangoma's feet.

"Hlalapanzi. Sit."

Emily heard Anna's footfall as Anna herself entered the cave. The water splashed over her and the baby. Emily sat down on the cold, stone floor and put her hand to her head. She looked into the sangoma's eyes. The one eye was dark brown, and the other a lighter gold colour. Or was it some strange reflection of light from the windscreen?

"IsiZulu," his voice boomed through the cave and Emily felt her heart race. She turned and looked at Anna.

"He wants to speak Zulu," Anna whispered. "I will interpret for you."

The sangoma's voice rose and fell in a sudden squall of sounds. With one swift move he gathered together the pile of objects in front of him and threw them out in an arc. His hands hovered over them, trembling, seeking, not touching. His eyes were closed. Emily bit her lip.

"You have an illness."

She knew that!

"There is danger that you will never carry a child. The illness is an illness of fear. You fear that which is in you, you fear the woman within you."

Emily shifted uncomfortably. The sangoma opened his eyes. They were moist and glassy. Though she looked right into them, she was convinced that he didn't see her. He stared out unblinking, his hands above the doll's arm.

"You have a great gift. You create images. I see images of death. You have been creating images of death. Change the image." He jumped up suddenly. "Care for the child. Care for the child and the earth and you will change the pattern of your illness. Do not anger your mother. The Earth Mother will nourish you. She ... will give you a name." Anna faltered in her interpretation, and looked at Emily. "Look to the Earth Mother for nourishment and do not let your fear grow ..." He clapped his hands and then spoke loudly in English. "Your English name ... Emily. Go now."

Emily stood and stumbled backwards. The sangoma was still staring through her into the distance. Sipho cried and Anna took him out of the cave. Emily ran after her, through the sunlit waterfall which fell over the mouth of the cave.

"Emily," Anna warned. "Slow down."

"Tell me the truth, Anna. Were you making up that stuff, or did he really say that?" Emily was breathless.

"Eh?"

"What does it all mean?"

"Just walk and we'll talk."

The sun was high in the sky and flocks of birds flew overhead. Far below in the distance, nestling between the trees, she saw the farmhouse and the thin wisp of smoke seeping from the chimney.

Sipho's face was squashed against Anna's back. *Care for the child* ...What did that mean?

"Maybe the sangoma gives that same speech to everyone who comes to him. Maybe it's up to the interpreter to make it mean whatever."

Anna didn't bother answering directly. She simply said: "If you follow his advice, you will recover. And more. You must take Sipho." She didn't sound happy.

Emily stopped dead in her tracks. "What?"

"He will be your responsibility."

That was crazy! Her legs shook as she stumbled down the steep mountainside. The sun-baked ground was hard as rock.

They walked the rest of the way in silence. Emily kept staring at Anna's back. What had the sangoma meant ... *Do not anger your mother?* Maybe he was confused. Surely he should have said: Don't let your mother anger *you!*

Emily sank down to sit in the cool of the veranda, leaning against the wall. She heard Uncle Tim cough as he rounded the house. Smile lines creased the skin around his eyes.

"How was it? You two go up the mountain?"

"Yip," Emily sighed. "Some walk." She was exhausted, but she thought gladly about the number of calories she must have burnt in those hours of walking and sweating. Now she could perhaps have something small to eat.

december 29th
the sangoma has no flipping IDEA what he was talking about. sipho is asleep in his crib in MY room. i wonder if i will ever sleep again ... could be i'm losing my mind and this a joke on me played by the world who are laughing only i think it is real and take it seriously ... supper i ate corn chips 140 calories for a serving (oh heavens!) and they have 7 grams of fat. will somebody please turn off this game show so that i can be myself again and not think i'm going crazy? what on earth did i think i was doing going to a man in jeans sitting in a cave behind glass with a pile of junk who said TAKE CARE OF THE CHILD? well anyway i'm doing it so somewhere i am not quite convinced that this is as nutty as i would LIKE to believe. goodnight. maybe for some time.

Chapter 6

Joey led the horse towards the outcrop of rocks above the dam. Emily went after him. Her stomach was full and she fought a wild urge to make herself vomit up the lunch she had eaten. The horse whinnied and stomped and Joey whispered in its ear.

"It's my fault," Emily said. "She can smell my frustration."

"No, she can't," Joey said. "But I can."

Sipho was asleep on the veranda and Anna was working in the house. The crib was covered with a light cloth and he slept at last. Emily could hardly keep her eyes open.

"I swear this is going to kill me," Emily said. "Look, Joey, I'm sorry but I can't go riding with you today."

Emily had planned to ride double-back with Joey up the mountain, but she was dropping with exhaustion. At least now the horse wouldn't have to carry both her and Joey up the mountain. She would let Joey go alone, she decided, then she would go back to the house and sneak in a few moments of sleep.

"Want to tell me exactly what's been going on?" Joey asked. He picked a long stem of grass and began chewing on it.

"I just feel like I haven't slept for a hundred years. And I can't get Sipho to eat. He won't take anything.

Not goat's milk, not porridge. It's terrible. I think he's got malnutrition. He doesn't look normal ... He's so tiny."

Joey was silent for a moment. Then he rubbed his dry hands together. "I understand," he said.

"I guess I'll see you later then, Joey."

"I guess." He looked disappointed. His eyes stared at her vacantly as if there was nothing left he could do. His lips moved as though he wanted to say something, but he just put up his hand and waved. Then Emily turned and began to walk back to the house.

She found Sipho awake in his crib on the veranda. He was staring up at the sky, his eyes moving as though searching for something. His tiny nostrils flared and Emily looked with a strange feeling of warmth at the small peppercorn curls on his head. She reached out her hand and prodded his arm. "Hey, I wish you would eat, kiddo," she whispered.

It was already dark when Uncle Tim came in. Emily was in the lounge holding Sipho. On the table was an apple, half-eaten, and a glass of milk. Beside the glass stood a bowl of cold, weak baby porridge. She rocked Sipho from side to side and didn't immediately see her uncle in the doorway.

"One mouthful, Sipho, is that all? Jeez, kiddo, I'm meant to be taking care of you. Why won't you eat?"

She gave a start when her uncle cleared his throat behind her. "Hi," he said. "Tired?"

"Can't even stand any more," Emily replied.

"Me too." He walked through the door and sat

down. Then he raised his eyes to his niece. "Joey went home. His father's village has been burnt down."

Emily's eyes widened. "What? But I saw him this afternoon. He looked a bit tense, but he didn't say anything!"

"No? Well, I don't know why. He's been worried about this happening for some time. His father is okay, but their fields have been torched, they've lost some livestock and they will have a hard time trying to get things started again."

"Why didn't I ... why didn't Joey ... say something?" She was speaking half to herself. She remembered the hollow look in his eyes when she said she wouldn't go riding. And then she felt a terrible sense of guilt. He had wanted to tell her. That was the whole purpose of riding up the mountain. So that they could talk. She thought about how his lips had moved and no sound had come out.

"I suppose Joey's not really one for talking about his own affairs," Uncle Tim said. But Emily knew differently. He had told her things about himself that no one else knew.

Sipho was breathing softly now, asleep. He was so light that all Emily felt on her shoulder was the warmth where his head rested.

"No one was hurt in the attack," Uncle Tim went on. "They believe it was motivated by jealousy. They had fertile ground and a good yield, while other relatives were less well-off. These things happen." He rubbed the bridge of his nose, looking very tired.

night
i am ashamed to say that i did not give joey the
chance to tell me that something awful had
happened to his father's fields. it was so selfish of
me to think only about myself. i haven't seen
anna today. sipho ate a spoonful of porridge and
drank a tiny bit of goat's milk. while i, on the
other hand, ate for two. tonight i am so tired that
i imagine i'll sleep through anything. i feel
disgusted with myself. about everything.

Emily was caught in a soft downpour as she hurried from the washing line to the back of the farmhouse. Sipho's sudden cry reached her, and she dropped the damp clothes in alarm. She nearly tripped on a squawking chicken on the back stairs as she dashed inside. Reaching the lounge door, she saw that the cushion on which Sipho had been sleeping was empty. Her heart gave a sudden lurch, and in that terrible moment she realized something with absolute clarity: Sipho had become a part of her. The thought of anything happening to him made her sick. She rushed into the room. He had rolled off onto the floor and was lying some way away with a blanket tangled over his head.

"Oh, jeez, I'm so sorry. Kiddo, I'm so careless. I had no idea you could move like this. Nobody told me." She pulled the blanket from his face and picked him up gently. His body was soft and she held it against her, rubbing her cheek against his head. Slowly his crying stopped. "Hey, Sipho," she whispered. "Maybe this wasn't such a bright idea ... that witch doctor of yours didn't reckon with the hazards of some stupid kid taking care of you." His head went back as she spoke and he wrinkled up his nose. Emily looked at the tiny boy and her heart opened to him.

Rain drummed steadily on the roof and Emily propped Sipho on a pile of pillows so that he was half-sitting. His body flopped over to the side and she steadied him. Then she took the piece of paper that was sticking out of the medical book and looked at it thoughtfully. She reached for her crayons and put the paper down in front of Sipho. What was this? The picture looked so dark and solemn. Was that art? Skeletons and pyramids and the birth of 5000-year-old withered bodies? She ran to the shelf and pulled her sketchbook from amongst Uncle Tim's literature. She set herself up in front of Sipho and began to draw ... the contour of his cheek, the softness of the face ... the huge eyes, opened wide.

She drew and erased, and blew the paper so that bits flew off onto the floor. And then suddenly she had the picture of the sangoma's face right in front of her as clear as if she had been staring at him, and she could hear Anna's voice: *You have been creating images of death. Change the image.*

A shudder shook Emily's whole body. Was *this* what he had meant? Her drawings? Her heart beat loud in her ears and Sipho flopped over to the side again. Emily gently lifted him back with one arm while the other arm continued to shade in the curve of his cheek. She was trying to capture him forever, freeze him in time in grey lead pencil.

i have not slept well for i don't know how many
nights. i have learnt once and for all to trot and
even canter. sipho is still not eating well. my mom
(how do i say this again) is now with someone
new. PETER. ANOTHER *surfer. sipho is still too small*
and weak. on the other subject: it sounds as
though PETER *is just about the lowest form of life*
you could find on planet earth. hope mother
doesn't go so low as to worship those surfer's feet
which will probably stand on her before the week
is out.

Emily woke to the sound of a branch scratching against her window, and she sat up with a fright. Joey's shadowy face peered through the glass.

"Oh!" She crawled out of bed, pulling her blanket with her. Joey beckoned to her. She opened the window.

"Is Sipho still sleeping?" he whispered.

"Yes, and I also just fell asleep." She rubbed her eyes. Her bones felt like lead. The morning was misty and the whole farm was covered by a white haze.

"There's a whisper in the wind," Joey said.

"What on earth are you talking about?"

"The Spirit of the Mountain has grown uncomfortable. The horses told me, and I've smelt it."

"Wait," Emily said. "Wait just a moment." She pulled her curtains shut and hastily dressed herself. Then she ran outside to meet him. Smoke curled up into the sky from the stone chimney of the farmhouse.

"I heard about your father," she said. "And I'm sorry that ..."

"It's okay," he said hurriedly. "But I'm talking about something else."

"I don't understand," Emily said. "Why can't you talk about it normally?"

"It isn't like that. I mean it, something is going to happen here. Come to the stables and see what I mean."

Emily's feet were icy cold as she walked across the farm. Mist swirled around them in faint curls and spirals. The horses stood uneasily at the edge of the paddock. As Joey approached, one of them stomped and his ears went back. Joey put out his hand and Emily kept a slight distance. Then his hand touched the horse's muzzle and the horse pushed up against him with such force that he stumbled backwards. Emily's breath caught in her throat. Joey whispered to the horse. The grass at her feet rustled. What if a snake was the cause of all the excitement? She was uncomfortably aware that she was standing there, stupidly, barefoot.

Joey walked over to Emily. His eyes had that strange colour to them again. It was as though they were flecked with gold. As he brushed his hair from his eyes, Emily's heart turned a slow, lazy somersault and a strange feeling spread through her belly. Suddenly, for no apparent reason, the whole world felt different.

"Listen," Joey said. "There's something in the air — something is going to happen. Come with me. I want to show you the Spirit of the Mountain."

"I'm a bit ... scared," Emily said, and her voice sounded weak. "You're making me shake. What's going to happen, Joey? How can you be so sure?" She met his eyes and nervously put her hand to her hair, weaving it between her fingers.

"Something's brewing. I don't know. Animals see and hear things that we don't. Come with me up the mountain and you'll understand."

Emily bit her lip. She was torn. She shook her head.

"I can't. Not today. I have to be with Sipho. You know he's just about eating ... he's beginning to trust me."

"You could ask Anna to help," he said.

"I know. But I've decided not to. This is my responsibility. You have to understand that."

"Fine," Joey said. His voice was calm as always, but Emily knew from the way he squared his shoulders that it was not fine, and that he was hurt. Once more she was doing something else when she could have been with him. He turned his head away and began to walk, quickly, head down, through the mist towards the stables.

Emily stood shivering in the grass. Her feet were so numb she couldn't feel them. The air was thick and white and the sky seemed to have fallen right to the ground. A strange panic overcame her and she hurried in what she hoped was the direction of the farmhouse. It appeared suddenly, through the mist in front of her. She sat on the veranda steps with her head in her hands. She took deep breaths until the pounding in her head eased.

Gradually the mist cleared and the day turned hazy and warm. The sun peered through the whiteness at odd intervals. Emily watched Sipho sleeping. He lay between two sheets, his head to the left, his arms stretched up above his shoulders. His legs were spread out, relaxed under the sheets. Emily bent to listen to his shallow breathing, and felt his soft, warm breath on her cheek. She paced across the room.

Uncle Tim arrived with the evening. He had grass in his hair and smudges of dirt down his face. He had obviously had a hard day at work.

"Em?"

"Yip?"

"Would you like to join us? We're making a fire out there behind the stores, and having a braai. A kind of cook-out which we do once in a while to give everyone on the farm a hearty meal and the chance to be loud and noisy with each other."

"Loud and noisy in Zulu?"

"Mostly."

Emily hung her head. She wondered whether Joey would be there. If he would even speak to her. "Nah. I'll stay at the house."

"Anna said she'll take care of Sipho tonight."

"Why?"

"So you and I can go there together." He rubbed his beard. He had sand under his fingernails.

"Okay," said Emily. "I'll come. Is it safe, Uncle Tim?"

"What do you mean?" he smiled. "Of course. Don't let stories scare you."

"But things are happening around here, aren't they?"

"Yes," he said thoughtfully. "But sometimes they aren't as simple as they appear to be. Fear doesn't help."

Uncle Tim led the way through the shadows towards the sound of laughter and a crackling fire. She could smell the cooking meat.

"What animal?" she asked.

He chuckled. "Em, don't ruin my appetite."

"Hey, we might as well face facts. Meat is animal, but dead. So what is it?"

"Lamb," he replied.

"Yuk."

"You can eat the baked potatoes."

"Thanks. D'you think Joey will be here?"

"I haven't seen him all day. I imagine he will, though. Is something wrong? You sound awfully pensive."

"Joey's upset with me. Because I wouldn't go up the mountain with him. Well, he can jolly well be upset if he likes!" she said, and then realized she'd spoken out loud what she'd meant to keep to herself.

Beyond the smoke the night was deep and sprinkled with stars. The smoke drifted up in an orange swirl against the Milky Way. Flames leapt up, crackling. They seemed to snap the laughter and chatter in two. It was a wide sky, Emily thought, a blanket of jewels over them all, protecting them. Then she frowned in the dark. Her jeans were feeling tighter. She had been eating too much and if she didn't watch out, she would grow fat all over again and have to starve all over again. Better to catch it now. No potatoes then, or anything else. No breakfast either. Nothing until the jeans loosened to what they were before.

Warmth from the fire reached her and she saw the dark glistening faces of the workers next to the flames.

Some were smiling, others were serious. They were drinking and she could smell the strong, homemade beer. The night was full of noises. Emily thought once that she caught a glimpse of Joey, but if it was him, he quickly disappeared.

"Beer?" Uncle Tim offered.

"No, thanks. Not me."

Suddenly there was a commotion. People scattered. Emily heard a loud cry and an outburst of Zulu. Uncle Tim pushed past the people in front of them. There was a thud as something landed in the crowd next to the fire. Then there were screams and Emily saw a flash of what looked like steel in the firelight. Then she could clearly see Joey standing at the centre, his foot on the back of a youth who lay on the ground. Joey shouted and men rushed forward. There were four of them, each holding a prisoner in his sweaty grasp. Uncle Tim pushed Emily back. "Move it," he kept saying. "Just move it."

Before she rushed away she saw that Joey's dark face was a mask of horror. He gripped the boy lying at his feet. His foot rested on the boy's wrist, which still limply grasped a long, sharp, glittering panga knife.

31st december
they were on this farm, and would have DONE
something for sure. anna says they are angry
because uncle T gave a job to one guy but really
his brother needed the job and was older and was
angry so got his friends together to come and
attack. who? jeepers, i don't know, US! joey SMELT out

the guy. said he arrived at the fire and smelt a
foreigner (could have been me, i said). no, he knew
who it was, he said, and went for him. he shouted
that there were others in the bushes and then the
workers from the farm caught all but one and tied
them up and kept them in the stables all night.
(crumbs, YOU try and sleep with this going on!) and
of course anna and everyone, also joey, slept in the
house. this morning i was so hungry i ate breakfast
and went and actually made myself bring up (it
was easy). last night could have been a farewell
party for all of us to planet earth ... no this is not
funny. well, i have been eating out of necessity, BUT
gotten rid of the food OTHERWISE. except for the
chappies chewing gum i ate. DID YOU KNOW? JUPITER
HAS 14 SATELLITE MOONS AROUND IT. DID YOU KNOW? JUPITER
IS THE LARGEST OF THE PLANETS. DID YOU KNOW? MERCURY
TAKES ONLY 88 DAYS TO ORBIT THE SUN. BUT did you know
that chappies (enough of them) can make you FAT?
nobody told me that one, ha ha, i agree this is not a
time to be funny but in case i get killed, i don't want
these diaries to be found and read and then the
diagnosis reached that i was a depressed, mentally
unstable teenager who would have killed herself
anyway. good afternoon ladies and gentlemen and
thank you for listening in once again. we hope that
the lack of capital letters in the show has not
impaired your hearing ... ha ha ... STOP.

Chapter 7

It was early evening and Emily walked with Joey through the trees to the river. She had not been there since the day she had fallen. She saw the grass and leaves and the pebbles under the clear water as if she had never seen them before.

"So what happened after that?" Emily asked.

"I was afraid, you know, not for myself, but because I had smelt it in the air beforehand. As if something were burning."

"Tell me again about the others."

"We tied them up, and this morning I went with the men and we took them to the sangoma. He said that they had come to commit an injustice and had to be punished. He made them carry rocks all day from the foot of the mountain to the top, to build an enclosure for the goats that belong to one of the villagers."

Emily shook her head and looked up at Joey. He had very white teeth when he smiled, but his smile was rare. She licked her lips.

"I'm not the city kid you think I am, Joey. I also believe that there are things that are real that we can't necessarily see. But I didn't want to, 'cos it's unsettling."

Joey looked at her out of the corner of his eye and then sat down on the grass. "Where's Sipho?"

Emily smiled and played with her lip. "Sleeping. Being babysat by Uncle Tim."

"Did he offer?"

"No, I asked."

"But you're still sick, aren't you?"

"You don't know anything about this, Joey."

"Why don't you try me? You never talk about yourself."

"I eat like a pig, Joey. I eat such a lot. Then I get rid of it. I'm caught in it and I don't know how to stop. But I know I can't stop, or I'll get fat." Emily herself was surprised by her sudden confession.

"What I suppose I find hard to understand, is that you think there's something wrong with being fat, or plump, that is, and ..."

"I thought you understood," Emily said, her eyes narrowing as she stood up. "You haven't a clue!"

"I haven't finished ..." he called. She walked away from him through the golden evening. She pushed aside branches touched with the fading glow of the sun. The river's gurgle faded and she saw the huge shadow of the mountain in front of her. The moon was already out, a papery sliver in the sky. It was white and almost transparent, like the smudged clouds on the horizon.

Her breath came in short gasps and Emily carried on towards the distant stables. In her mind she saw the hunched figure of the 5000-year-old man get up slowly, trying to move. His limbs were withered, his legs stiff. She could smell his age; his grin was half that of a man, half that of a skeleton. He was made of earth and of bone. He looked ...

"Emily!" Joey had run after her and he grabbed her arm just as she was about to fall. "Listen. Listen to me please! You look like walking death. It's horrible."

Emily collapsed, crumpling into a ball. It felt better

that way. She blinked her eyes and tried to rid herself of the picture of the ancient man. Weakly she pulled her arm out of Joey's grasp.

"Leave me alone," she whispered. "Please."

The last glow of the sun faded and the first stars twinkled in the sky. Emily sat with Anna on the veranda. She had stumbled home and asked for a glass of orange juice, which Anna had given her. It revived her and she sat looking out over the farm, shaking her head. "Anna, it's just not working."

"What?" Anna asked, and looked at her.

"Everything. It's not helping me. The sangoma's plan, or your ideas. Although I love Sipho, I can't look after him properly. He's eating a bit, Anna, and it got me eating too, but now I do worse things to myself. I can't look after him any more. I can't take care of him any longer. How can I look after someone else when I don't even know how to look after myself?" She bit her nails. Somewhere in the distance, goats bleated. "And I've just made the biggest fool of myself," she said glumly. "I got upset with Joey and ran away from him. I'll never be able to look him in the eye again."

Anna didn't say anything. She simply looked at Emily.

"Anyway," Emily said, "I'm not really myself. I'm frazzled by all the stuff going on around here, you know? People being murdered. People creeping around with knives and spears. And the city is worse. I can't see myself going back there. School starts in a week and a half. There is nothing for me to go back to."

"You should apologize to Joey," Anna said finally.

Emily rubbed her eyes. Then she shook her head glumly.

new year's day
and what a happy new year it is! phone call
from mother dear: are you well and are you
eating? oh and when are you coming back? joey
hasn't said a word to me. i've seen him cleaning
the stables all by himself and have not offered
any help. i'm waiting for him to do something.
well ladies and animals i overheard uncle Tim
talking to mom on the telephone this morning:

uncle T: yes, she's fine ... no not yet ... a coloured
boy? meryl, don't concern yourself over that
okay? it's perfectly all right no I'm afraid i
don't think that would help no, we haven't been
affected directly though there was some
excitement on the farm ... all taken care of.

it went something like that tho' i think there
was some other stuff about mother wanting to
visit here — hardly likely — there is a fat spider
on the wall next to me. it comes out every night
to eat mozzies. uncle T said something to my
mom about joey — boy i can just feel her
thoughts coming in through my windows.

The drawing lay in front of Emily and she stared at the white space in the corner of the page. The house was empty. Sipho was with Anna and Emily looked at her copy of his face in pencil. She heard Uncle Tim come in through the kitchen door. He put a pot of water on the stove and the pipes in the wall chugged as he turned on the hot-water tap to wash his hands.

"You in there, Em?"

"Uh-huh."

The drawing was degenerating as she tried to make Sipho's face more like Sipho. She could not get his likeness at all. There was something that escaped her. Perhaps she just wasn't talented enough. In the lounge, insects ticked against the wall and banged into the lightbulb overhead. A moth was trying to destroy itself on the bulb, darting towards it again and again. At last Emily jumped up, catching the moth in her hand. She ran to the window and hurled the creature out into the night. "Idiot!" she said as it disappeared into the dark.

Uncle Tim came into the room and rubbed his nose. He lifted his eyebrows and said: "I have some news for you."

"What kind of news?"

"A woman was here earlier. She claims to be Sipho's mother."

Emily's heart stopped beating for an instant. "How do you mean?"

"She arrived from a village over the hill. She said that Sipho was stolen by her husband who claimed that his wife bore someone else's child. So he took the baby and dumped it. Now he's vanished and the woman has found out about Sipho. She wants to see him."

"Jeepers, Uncle Tim!" Her stomach suddenly ached.

"Well, she's coming tomorrow if you want to see her," Uncle Tim said. "There's always the chance, of course, that she isn't his mother at all. But under these circumstances that seems highly unlikely."

"Oh yes. I want to see her," Emily nodded.

In the dim morning light Emily saw the figure of a woman standing on the stairs outside Anna's rondavel. Anna had had Sipho with her these last few nights, because Emily had been too weak to wake up in the middle of the night. Uncle Tim was wearing his tan leather jacket. His breath made white puffs in the still air as he walked towards Anna's house. The morning smelt of smoke. A door creaked and opened. They waited expectantly, but Anna didn't come out. Slowly Emily let her eyes fall on the woman hesitating outside the open door. She was round and tall, with a full, moon-shaped face. Her eyes seemed heavy and she kept them fixed on the ground. Uncle Tim said a few words to her in Zulu. He spoke slowly, haltingly. She answered quickly. Her voice was soft and direct. Then he turned to Emily.

"She tells me her baby was taken from her at two weeks. That he was a boy."

Anna appeared in the doorway. Her eyes fell on the woman. Emily held her breath. Anna frowned. The woman spoke softly in Zulu and Anna nodded. She beckoned and the woman followed her into the rondavel.

"See what happens," Uncle Tim said. He shrugged. The air was chilly and Emily shivered. She shut her eyes to keep out the face of the woman who could be

Sipho's mother. The face made her feel sad. She held her hands to her own small, bony face and pressed her fingers to her cheekbones, feeling them under her eyes. She touched the place that protruded, hard and skeleton-like. *You look like walking death*, Joey had said. Could it be true? Cattle lowed on the hillside and dogs barked through the trees. Then suddenly the door of the rondavel opened and the woman emerged.

Perhaps tears shone in her eyes, or perhaps she was simply angry. Her whole body was taut and she muttered in Zulu. Then she looked at Emily for one full, confusing second, and swung around. She walked furiously through the grass until she disappeared behind a copse of trees.

"What?" Emily spoke nervously to Uncle Tim. He ran his hand through his hair. He shook his head. Anna didn't come out of the rondavel.

"So I guess that's not the last we'll see of her," Emily ventured to say. She wasn't quite sure what had just happened.

"You may be right," Uncle Tim agreed.

There was something wrong about the way in which the woman had left. It seemed as though she was ... threatening. Emily felt a pang go through her. Perhaps the woman wasn't Sipho's mother, but if she was, and if Anna had chased her away ... The imprint of the woman's face stayed in her mind. Sipho's mother. She was sure. The woman was Sipho's mother.

"Uncle Tim?" Emily asked seriously.

"Mmm?"

"Tell me. D'you think Joey thinks that I think that he's different because he's not ... white?"

"I don't know if I got that."

"Yes you did!"

"You're asking *me* for advice?"

"Kind of."

"Oh, advice, how I love to advise. Now let me think. You are in quite a bad way, Em," he said. "Have you looked in the mirror lately?"

She turned her head and looked out at the hills. The woman was gone, swallowed up by the blue-grey mountain swells.

"Ah, I thought not. Well, you see, maybe you don't see how hard it is for people to watch you slowly destroying yourself. Bit by bit, every day you are vanishing. And not to be able to do anything about it is very hard. Maybe for a minute I can put some people in front of you. Okay, your mother. Yes, she's neurotic, but she is your mother, and she loves you. Anna, who was prepared to do anything for you if it would help, even gave Sipho over to your care ... no mean feat, she felt very attached to the child. Then Joey. I don't think he cares whether you're black, white or green, but how would you feel if someone you were starting to care about was slowly killing themselves, and every time you saw them you saw less and less of the person they actually were? Wouldn't that destroy you?

"Oh, and there's me, I suppose. I thought that merely by being here, having something else to think about, you would get well. Not so simple, huh? But I do not admit defeat. Not yet. No matter how much the problems are out there, they are also in here," he touched his heart, "and you have to find a way to help the people who love you, because if you can't, their hearts will be broken. I never dreamt that I could lecture like this. I won't again, but I had to get this off my chest, see?"

When he turned his face to her, his cheeks were flushed and his eyes were shining. She fought hard to swallow a lump in her throat.

january midnight somewhere between the 2nd and the 3rd
the world is doing a headstand and i am at the
bum end of everything, yessir it's all cracked open,
me and the whole country and joey and anna ...
sipho's mother came looking for him, at least i think
it could be her but anna kept him. she told the
mother i was taking care of him according to the
wishes of the sangoma. how can i help? he has a
serious health problem. anna should just give him
back to the woman who wants him. this is going
wrong. things have gone to rot so much. well, ladies
and mosquitoes, this is the midnight show. school
starts next week. i dreamt of eating dog food.
calories and calories of grossness, but could not stop,
oh it was SO gross. and i am not talking to joey. he
hasn't spoken to me and that woman looked so hurt
and angry as she walked away ... i am scared. this
is not a game. that could be his MOTHER. well folks,
that's all from this end of hell. here's looking at you,
world, through mud and other murky substances.

Emily slept restlessly, tossing and turning in her bed and waking late in the night to find her sheets tangled about her. She looked up. The moon shone eerily through her window and cast shadows of leaves and branches on her wall. A breeze blew in through the window and she sat up. She had forgotten to close the curtains and was still dressed in her jeans. Her diary lay open on the wooden table next to her bed and the pages fluttered in a gust of wind.

She climbed out of bed and walked towards the window. The night was huge, it had a presence. The moon shone above the ridge of a mountain and cast a silver line across the contours. Emily caught her breath. In the glow she could make out the features of a giant face. She saw the high brow, the nose, the full lips. The face extended the entire width of the mountain. It looked as though it was sleeping. Was she dreaming? She shivered and her knees knocked together. She was very much awake. The moon dipped behind the mountain and the contours were lit even brighter for a moment. Emily took a shaky step backwards. The face was so huge, so proportionately perfect. How could she not have seen it before? Was this what they meant? Was this the Spirit of the Mountain? How was it possible that something in nature could copy a human face so exactly? Or was there something out there, some SPIRIT, and people and mountains were just copies of IT? Emily swallowed. A moment passed and the scene in front of her darkened as the land was plunged into a cool, moonless predawn.

Chapter 8

The car rumbling up the farm road took Emily by surprise. She bent low over the newly dug earth and wiped the sweat from her brow. It was late in the morning and the sun shone obscurely through white, drifting clouds. The mountains were clear and seemed a lot closer than they actually were. Emily turned her head but could not see any trace of that mysterious midnight face. She had earth beneath her nails. She was learning how to plan according to the cycles of the moon. The garden would be planted with vegetables and herbs, enough that Uncle Tim would be able to sell them and make a profit. Emily closed her eyes as she recognized the car. Her heart sank. It was Saturday. School would start on Monday. The car door slammed and her mother patted her dress and walked across the grass to the veranda. Emily kept low and watched her mother. She looked pale and lifted her hand to tap on the front door.

Emily waited for her mother and Uncle Tim to emerge from the house and come over to the area where she was working, but they didn't. She went to the small basket in which Sipho slept, covered by a mosquito net and in the shade of a tree. He had brought up the milk that she had tried to feed him. Suddenly her heart stood still. Across the path she saw Anna. She was carrying an armful of freshly picked thyme to be packed away in the storeroom.

"Anna?" she called out. She dusted her hands and ran towards her. "Anna, you won't believe it — my mother's here!"

"Is she? That's good," Anna nodded.

"No," Emily said and shook her head. "She's going to freak. Look at me!" Emily looked down at her dirty clothes and then she looked at the sleeping baby. "Oh," she groaned. "Anna, you can't be seen with me."

Anna frowned and put down her bundle of herbs. Then she rested her hands on her hips. "I know," she said. "I'll take care of Sipho. You have to be strong, Thandiwe."

"What did you just call me?"

"Thandiwe. Your Zulu name."

"I don't have a Zulu name."

"You do now."

"What does it mean?"

"Aha!" Anna picked up the bundle again and adjusted the scarf on her head. She lifted the covering over Sipho's crib. They both peered in at the sleeping baby. His mouth had a slight white ring around it. His eyelids fluttered in his sleep and his hands lay stretched above his head. He breathed heavily. Emily swallowed a lump in her throat. Why wouldn't he eat? His mother should be with him, trying to feed him. How could Anna keep him from his own mother? She rocked back unsteadily on her feet. Anna looked at her and pulled Sipho's basket closer.

"Go inside to your mother."

Her mother was sitting on a chair in the lounge, nervously tapping her foot. Uncle Tim sat opposite.

"Hi, Mom." Emily took another step into the room.

"Timothy says you've started a garden."

"Yip."

"How is it going?"

"Okay, I suppose. I've only just started."

Her mother's face changed, her eyes shifted.

Emily sat down and twirled her hair between her thumb and forefinger. She looked out of the window at the hills, folded and crumpled like fabric in the hands of some careless giant. She was dreaming. Uncle Tim walked with her mother into the kitchen and put on the kettle for tea. Vaguely she could hear their conversation.

"... have been very difficult for me ... am not checking up on you, Timothy ... needed to see her ... rethought the way our lives have been lived ... very difficult and moody ... Oh, I know you don't think so, but you don't live with her ..."

They walked back into the lounge and Emily looked squarely at her mother. "Why did you come here?"

Her mother looked flustered. "I ... well, I thought I'd come and see for myself how you're doing, that's all."

"Why didn't you tell me you were coming?"

Her mother flicked imaginary dust from her dress. She put her hand to her brow. Emily wanted to hand her a cigarette or something, so that she would at least know what to do with her hands.

"I just couldn't ... didn't want to hear you say that you didn't want me to come here. That's all."

"It's a good idea that you two talk for a while," Uncle Tim said and stood up.

Emily threw a pleading glance in his direction. She didn't feel like this, not now, not in a million years. She didn't want to hear how hard it had been for her mom, how her sickness was making her mother sick. She was thinking too about the sangoma's warning that she should not anger her mother.

"Can I see your garden?" her mom asked. Emily was taken aback.

"Okay. You sure you can walk in those shoes?"

"I'll try."

They went out of the kitchen door. Heat pressed down on them — heavy, viscous, sticky. The sky stretched out overhead, far into the distance, a giant arc of blue.

The sand showed red where Emily had been digging. Anna must have taken Sipho back with her to her rondavel. She saw her mother's face twitch.

"Aren't there workers to do this sort of thing?"

"The whole point is for me to do it myself. Partly this is because of the sangoma."

"What are you talking about, Emily?"

"I went to see the sangoma, and he said that I should ..."

"I don't believe this. Have you gone crazy?" Her mother's voice trembled. "These people, Emily, are barbarians. They'll kill you or ... or ..."

"Enough," Emily said angrily. "Stop it. You just don't understand."

"You're quite right. I'm trying, I really am. But this is the limit. My daughter, seeing a *witch doctor*. Emily, now listen to me. I want you to come home with me tomorrow morning." She was struggling to keep her voice even. "Come back and let's get our lives back to normal." Her voice was low and strained.

Emily wished she had kept her big mouth shut. She should have known a million times better than to mention the sangoma. Her mother scratched her leg and laddered her thin stocking. Irritated, she pulled her shirt tighter around her waist and tried to keep her hair out of her face. It was a steamy, sticky day, and Emily felt good in it. She drew in a breath and whistled out through her teeth. "The truth is," she said without looking at her mother. "I have to stay here. I can't leave because I'm responsible for too much right now." Her mother scraped the bottom of her eyelid with a long fingernail and rolled her eyes to the sky. Emily saw the whites of her eyes only and looked away.

"I'm not ready to go back," Emily said. "I'm not leaving this place. Not now."

Her mother stood in grass that brushed her ankles. The wind tangled her hair and blew it into her eyes. "I know about the incident," she said. "About the boys with their knives. It's dangerous here. You could get killed. I want you to come home."

"Is that why you came here? Just to take me home?"

"Yes."

midnight january 5th
my mom asleep on the spare bed in lounge with
nocturnal spider (unseen by her) crouching up in
corner of roof, staring down at her wondering if
to bite or not. skin probably not sweet enough.

well, ladies and whatsits, don't think about joey,
because i'm trying not to. the show is on a bit late
tonight because the airwaves were muddled for a
long time and no communication was possible. my
mom says she has not done a good job as a
mother and then in the same breath but why am i
just such a DIFFICULT *teenager? (oh those faultless*
girls on the covers of magazines ... if only every
girl had such legs and hair). to top it all i
overheard my mom say to T that i was looking a
*little better (*FATTER*?) than when i left. crumbs*
crumbs oh help. i see in front of me my face
getting fatter and fatter like a huge balloon and
then one day it will burst. hope you're protected
from spiders and other creepycrawlies lurking,
plotting etc.

Early the next morning, Emily heard footsteps in the kitchen and climbed out of bed to open her curtains. She tiptoed through to the lounge where her mother was still asleep. Anna was boiling a big pot of water on the stove. Sipho was tied to her back, his head turned towards her. She smiled at him, looked him in the eye and whispered: "Hey, kiddo. Are you going to have something to eat today? Please?" then she looked up at Anna.

"Want some porridge, Thandiwe?"

"N ... no thanks."

"I saw Sipho's mother," Anna said.

"You did?"

"I was walking back from the sangoma yesterday and I saw her down at the river, washing clothes. I followed her and kept at a distance till I saw which village she went to. Then I crept closer. I saw her hut. I will watch her more."

"You mean spy?"

"Yes."

"What for?"

"Just to see."

"Why, Anna?"

"Because I want to know about her."

Emily looked at the baby's head, reached out and took his hand in hers. Then she stroked his soft skin. It was like silk, like talcum powder. She swallowed and rubbed her eyes.

"I can't be a mother to him, Anna. I'm only fifteen." Then she looked away. "What were you doing with the sangoma?"

"I took some of Sipho's hair. And when the woman came I touched her hand. I did not wash it or use it and went to the sangoma."

"And ..."

"He would not say anything. Not now."

"Why?"

"He says to wait."

"You listen to everything he says, don't you?"

"He speaks the truth."

Emily shook her head and leant on the kitchen dresser. She heard her mother shuffle and get up.

"Oh no, Anna. Quick, go."

"No. Now sit down and have some porridge."

"I said no. Please, Anna, if you don't go, she'll come in here and ..."

"Yes?"

A moment later her mother's head popped around the corner and Emily looked at her guiltily. She didn't know what her mother was thinking. By the way her eyes raked over Anna, she could tell that her mom wasn't pleased. Usually Emily would have run away from such a situation. But now she waited. She felt strong in her resolve. Anna was her friend.

"Mom, how did you sleep?"

"Fine." She was pale-faced. Anna stood stirring the pot, pouring in oats. Sipho opened one eye and stared out at Emily. She shifted and went over to him. She rubbed his back. Her mother seemed to flinch. Her heavily made-up eyes were half-closed. Her blonde, teased hair was tousled. She pulled a strand of hair behind her ear and shook her head. The yellow tiles on the floor gleamed brightly in the morning sun. Through the open window Emily heard roosters crow, goats bleat and saw the smoke of the fires in the distance. An uncomfortable silence hung between them. Emily shifted from one foot to the other. Nothing was going to happen. Her mother was pale and tense as she stared at Anna's hands which mixed and churned until the pot steamed and the smell of oats reached her nostrils. Her mother took in a breath and her voice was cool. "Well, Emily. I'm going."

Emily felt the blood leave her face as her mother left the room.

The car drove away from the house in the early afternoon and Emily stayed behind. Uncle Tim sat on the veranda steps with Emily and Sipho. She sighed and rubbed her head. "School starts without me. Mom goes home without me. I've made her angry. What am I doing?"

"Planting a garden and healing yourself. No time is wasted. There's nothing else to do except try and try and never give up. You have to get better."

Emily took Sipho into her arms. His body was still so light that she scarcely felt his weight. She shook up the bottle of milk and put it to his lips. He opened his mouth but choked and coughed the milk back out again. Emily felt anger rise in her. This was unfair. He would not eat, and *somewhere* he had a *mother* who wanted him *back*! And dear Anna, for all her wisdom and good will, was making life very difficult indeed.

There was tension in the air. It felt as though you could snap it with your fingers. Something was going to happen. Was she getting like Joey now? Smelling things in the air? In addition to all this, her jeans and shorts had been feeling tighter. She looked down at herself, rocking Sipho as she patted his back.

"Am I fatter?"

"Em, come on. Stop this."

"No, seriously, Uncle Tim. Tell me. Am I?"

"Don't be ridiculous. We can't discuss things in such terms, Em. Do you think of skeleton bones in terms of fat or thin? You're ill. Forgive me, but I've lost my sense of humour about this."

"Sorry."

"Now, I want to know if you would like to join Joey

and myself tonight. We're going on a hike up the mountain some time around midnight."

"I haven't spoken to Joey for a while, Uncle Tim."

"Has something happened?"

"It's just me. I'm all weird."

"Come with us anyway."

"What about Sipho?"

"Anna's here."

The sun set over the hills and Emily watched from the kitchen window. A half moon hung in the sky just above the horizon, fat and orange. It looked like half an egg. She heard a dog howl on a nearby farm and her stomach felt hollow. She wasn't sure what it would be like, seeing Joey again. Speaking to him. Her heart fluttered uncomfortably. She was hungry.

At ten o'clock Uncle Tim started bustling around the house. He filled a flask and packed a small backpack. He rustled up some warm clothes and threw a large, green jacket into Emily's room.

"Gets kind of cold up there," he said.

There was a knock at the door, and Emily's heart gave a light extra beat. Joey. She heard his voice and crept out of her room.

"Is that you, Emily?" Uncle Tim's voice called down the corridor. "Come on! We're all set to go."

Joey's face was cast in shadows as they started walking towards the hills. They wore jackets and jeans under the huge night sky. The grass rustled and they heard odd noises from the bush. No one carried a torch.

"Your eyes will grow accustomed to the dark," Uncle

Tim said. "If you use a torch, you make yourself blind. It's a fact. Just wait a few moments and you'll be able to see. We should have quite a bit of moonlight too."

They walked in silence for a while, a night wind blowing their hair. Emily cleared her throat. "Where are we going? Why are we doing this?"

"For fun."

"You must have another reason."

"Oh, I do. You'll see later. Look, here the incline is already noticeable. Watch out for rocks," her uncle said.

Joey walked ahead of them, not speaking. His jacket was as dark as the night sky. Emily realized from the slope of the ground that they had reached the foot of the hills. Behind them, faint golden lights from the house glimmered through the trees. Smoke hung in the air. Smoke and herbs. Beyond these hills what would you find? Were the people there afraid? Should they be?

The nearest town was Estcourt, where Uncle Tim went to get supplies every week. She had not left the farm itself. There had been a lot of to-ing and fro-ing on her behalf. Uncle Tim down to Durban, back up; her mother up to the farm, back down. It was crazy. Was she really that important to them? Why should they care? Emily sighed with a hint of a smile and shook her head. No, she was not sorry for herself, not in the slightest.

"Anna followed Sipho's mother. She knows where she lives," Emily offered into the darkness. She hoped

Joey would respond. She wanted to engage him, to break the coldness, only she didn't know how.

"Aha," Uncle Tim said. "And what did she find?"

"Oh, not much. Just where she lives. She wants to keep track. Are you worried about Sipho?"

Joey interrupted suddenly, and the sound of his voice made Emily warm around her ears. "Everybody is," he said.

Emily was quiet for a while as they stumbled up the increasing incline. The moon was blocked out by a rocky outcrop. There were noises in the grass, faint squeaks and faraway whines. Something with huge wings flapped low over them, beating the air so that it whooshed around their heads. Then it disappeared.

"Owl," Joey said.

The stars were clear and bright, piercing the sky with gold and silver. Emily hung her head back far enough to gain an impression of the mountain ahead of them, and its outline against the sky. It loomed up far larger than she had imagined it could be. Of course they were much closer to it now. At a certain point Uncle Tim stopped. "Listen," he said. "Some sort of wild cat."

In the bush nearby there was a low growl. Emily shivered. "What kind?"

"Some sort of karacul. Lynx."

"Dangerous?" Emily shook.

"Shh, no."

Some moments passed and then they continued. The incline levelled off and the moon appeared again as they rounded the outcrop. Suddenly Emily turned her head and caught her breath. Outlined by the silvery light of the moon, she saw, huge and forbidding, the face of a giant. The mountain beyond seemed to breathe. The face was perfect, full, three-dimensional. It was twice as large as when she had seen it through her window, and this time it was not merely a profile, but the whole face. Deep shadows showed the hollows beneath the eyes, the groove beneath the chin. The moon lit up the line down the centre of the nose and Emily let out a cry. "What *is* it?"

Joey said quietly, "The Spirit of the Mountain."

"Uncle Tim?" Emily asked in a small voice.

"So now you've seen it. Our mountain giant."

Could it be real, in the sense of people being real, physical, here, now?

They stood on the grassy slope next to rocks and scrub and thorn trees. Uncle Tim took the pack off his back. "Tea, anybody?"

The liquid was warm and comforting and Emily took small sips. It was sweet and she sat opposite Joey, craning her neck to look at the giant until her vision blurred and her eyes ached.

"You can only see him some nights, when the moon shines a certain way, usually close to midnight. He is the spirit of this land. A powerful spirit, called on by the sangoma, by other healers. He is a force to be reckoned with in this world. Capable of destruction when his laws are broken, capable of great healing when his powers are harnessed. He is not to be ridiculed or mocked." Uncle Tim nodded slowly to himself in the darkness.

The tone of his voice prevented any more questions. The Mountain Spirit. This couldn't be some trick of nature, some play of light and shadows.

The moon seemed to catch itself in the branches of a thorn tree and Uncle Tim stood up and began to walk away to the hillside.

Emily looked in his direction and then back at Joey. Joey's face was in shadow. He gripped his knees, hugging them to himself with both hands.

"So your mother was here."

"Came and went." She shook her head and bit her lip. "I've been awful, Joey. Jeepers, I wish I could take back the way I behaved to you."

"Forget it. It doesn't matter."

Stones tumbled in their direction as Uncle Tim scrambled up a rock behind them.

"What's he doing?"

"Trying to get a better view."

Joey's face was close to hers. So close that she could hear him breathing. The wind was chilly and she hugged her jacket tighter around herself. Her heart was beating hard. Her hand rested on her knee. Suddenly Joey's hand touched hers. It stayed there. Emily could hardly move. She could feel the rough, warm skin and then she leant over and lightly rested her head on Joey's shoulder.

january 9th
there are 2 mes and one is trying to help while
the other is doing everything it can to stop me
getting fat again and i, or rather I, am caught in

the middle of this FAT *fight. what should i do? i know what i would do: keep on doing this until i die. but I don't want to go on. I have to do something about it. joeyjoeyjoey makes Me want to eat, to be well again. i don't know why. something is cracking and breaking inside me. my sketches are really awful, indicating that my mind has turned to* ROT. *am i a person am I a person? i am falling through a huge hole in the sky and can't get up again cos i am so heavy there is nothing left to pull me up. there are two of me, an old me and a new* ME, *and one of them is going to disappear sooner or later, from the face of this earth. do you understand ladies and earthworms?*

The garden was cleared and planted and an irrigation system had been set up: Emily would walk past the rows of seedlings and pour water over them from an old watering can. It was not a particularly efficient system, but it was reliable. Sipho was tied to her back. She felt his warmth against her, his small cheek against her back. It was exhausting to work like that, but it burnt up more calories.

Emily dusted her hands and unwrapped her lunch package. She took out a hunk of freshly baked bread and a raw cucumber. The food tasted good, real. She ate it all and tried to fight the feeling of guilt that came over her. Now you will start getting fat, it said. No, I'll get healthy, she replied. She would get rid of all those calories in one minute. No, she would not do it. She wanted to resist. Food was nourishment. Some people didn't have any. She was one of the lucky ones. Don't bring it up, she pleaded with herself. Don't waste it. Think of Sipho.

"Hey, kiddo," she said softly, "maybe you should try some of this stuff. It beats the whatsits out of goat's milk."

Chapter 9

It was a strange, misty morning when Emily heard the horses neighing furiously from the stables. She walked outside. Behind her on the lounge floor she left a grey-and-white pencil drawing of the inside of a cave. The sangoma's cave as she remembered it, but with the same texture on the outside as she had used in her drawings of pyramids. There was something that tied the cave to the pyramids. Something.

The air outside felt as though it were weighed down by some heavy force. Emily could not quite tell what it was, but she had the sensation of thickness in her throat and in her mouth, and it pressed down on her eyes.

Emily went in search of Joey. She scraped back her hair and stepped onto the grass, walking towards the stables.

Suddenly there was a burst of noise. Emily heard the horses. Then, running at a wild speed, Joey came from the stables, his arms swinging crazily from side to side. His mouth was open. His hair was wild and his eyes flashed brilliant white in his dark face. Behind him came Anna. She was running, holding onto her head-scarf. Emily felt her heart go cold. She thought of Sipho, lying inside on the lounge floor, tucked between cushions. It had to be ...

"Call Timothy!" Joey yelled in Emily's direction.

It was as if someone had lit a fire in Emily's stomach. She ran into the house and out through the back towards the stores.

"Uncle Tim! Hurry! Something ... something's happening ... I ..."

His shadow appeared in the doorway. He was holding a spade. He dropped it and followed her immediately to the house. Once inside, Emily waited trembling in the kitchen.

"Stay inside ... with Sipho," he said.

"What's going on?" But she knew. It was some sort of attack. This was the end. Maybe the Panga Boys were back. This time in full force. Her lips were dry. Uncle Tim walked out through the front door. Emily went to the lounge to look at the baby.

"I don't know what's happening," she whispered to him. Without thinking she helped him hold the bottle to his lips and wasn't aware that he began to drink. That he swallowed and swallowed and that nothing spilt out of his mouth.

Emily heard a rushing sound and went over to the window. She could hear Joey talking urgently to Uncle Tim. What was happening? Then, through the clearing mist, she became aware of forms in the distance. She rubbed her eyes. Lining the horizon to the left of the stables stood a row of men and women. They were hardly moving but their spears waved from side to side. The people were singing. They began moving closer.

"Oh!" Emily put her hand to her mouth. "The end." But then, all at once, as though dawn broke inside her, she felt a strange calm spreading through her. It didn't matter. Nothing mattered. She saw now what it was that her drawings had tried to show: that whatever was true about being human would live on for always and always, even after you died. Bodies weren't everything. The human spirit was everything, and bodies would shed themselves from human spirits, be sloughed off in a million different ways over the centuries, just as they attached themselves to human spirits and grew from babies to adults.

"Sipho, it's okay," she said. "Here, let me hold you. I don't know what's going to happen, but it's okay."

She picked him up and crossed the floor, holding the bottle to his mouth. Then she walked onto the veranda. Uncle Tim was gone. Anna was on the stairs. "Go back inside!" she shouted at Emily.

"No, Anna. What's happening?"

Joey stepped out from behind a tree. He pointed to the lines of people moving in. "The villagers," he said. "From over the hill. I don't know what they want."

Their shadows looked terrifying. Emily held Sipho close. She saw Uncle Tim walking briskly towards her, and next to him walked a man who was old and dark, who carried a spear in his hand. His face was lined and his eyes seemed to be yellow where they should have been white. As he opened his mouth to speak, Emily noticed that he had no teeth at all. The old man pointed at her and spoke in Zulu.

Anna walked up to Emily and whispered to her: "He wants to speak to you."

Emily handed the baby to Anna and slowly descended the stairs. The mist that hung above them was gently evaporating. The old man kept his bony finger pointed at her. It trembled and he let out a string of words that Emily could not understand. All at once she saw Joey. He came over to where she was standing, chewing nervously on a piece of grass. He waved the stem in front of him like a metal detector.

"You need help," he said. "I'll translate." He repeated this in Zulu for the man and then stood squarely between Emily and the old man's bony finger. The man began to talk and Joey translated the guttural sounds.

"We have come to take the black child from you, white girl."

Emily bit her lip.

"You have no business with him. Give him back."

As Joey spoke, a murmur went through the crowd. There was a loud clash of metal on metal, and the people parted in the middle. A figure burst through the crowd. Dressed in full tribal costume, with skins and skin boots and his necklace of lion's teeth, was the sangoma. Emily hardly recognized him. His eyes shone and blazed. Underneath his tribal clothes she imagined he would be wearing his old, worn jeans, but he wasn't. He held up his hand. The old man who had been pointing at her stumbled backwards over a clump of grass. Emily found herself close to Joey.

Anna stood holding Sipho on the veranda, and Emily suddenly noticed, with a quick, backwards glance, that his bottle was empty. His bottle was *empty!* Sipho had finished the goat's milk.

The sangoma's voice boomed out across the hills. It

was a voice like thunder that came from somewhere so deep that the ground itself seemed to tremble.

"He said," Joey murmured, "that they have disobeyed the Spirit of the Mountain. They are not welcome with their weapons on this land. It is holy land. Don't they know? It is healing land. Don't they know?" Joey's voice was low. The sangoma's face looked very young and then very old. He opened his mouth again and the mist evaporated to show the clear blue sky overhead.

"He says, what do they mean by threatening anyone on this land? They are interfering with the cycle of nature. They do not understand. The white girl is ill."

There was a murmur that reached the edge of the crowd. Emily began to notice individual faces. Some people were interested. Some were angry.

"He says that the white girl would die, but for the woman. He means Anna," Joey added. "And he says the white girl would die but for the child. But it is because of the white girl that the child will live. Today the child ate properly for the first time, and when he returns to his village he will be well."

The sangoma's face shone with perspiration. Then her eyes fell on one figure standing at the front of the shuffling crowd. She recognized Sipho's mother, and her heart raced. Her eyes rested nervously on the thin, tattered dress that hung from the woman's shoulders. Her face was angry and in pain. The mother stood there for a long time. Her eyes never left Emily. Her mouth was downturned and her fists were clenched at her sides. The woman looked at the sangoma and her lips moved.

Somehow the sangoma had known that Sipho had eaten. A shiver ran down Emily's back.

The sangoma began to tap the ground with his feet, turning the sand to dusty clouds. He danced slowly, purposefully, every muscle in his body stretched and taut. And in the rhythm and repetition of his movement, Emily was at last able to feel its strength ... the sangoma's power that seemed suddenly to have descended on all of them. In silence he danced. And when his body was glistening and running with perspiration he stopped. The crowd moved back. They were talking in low voices, drifting away in a muffled hum and murmur. The heat began to rise from the ground and Sipho's mother disappeared into the crowd. As she did so, Emily heard a loud cry, a wail that went right to her heart.

> *january 11th*
> *next to me a child is sleeping and by the soft rise*
> *and fall of his chest i know that he is alive. so,*
> *today you ate. your stomach is full. there are*
> *expressions on your tiny brown face which make*
> *me believe that maybe you do know what is going*
> *on. i felt the power of the sangoma and i know*
> *that what he says, everyone will do. they are*
> *afraid of his magic. i'm afraid too. tho' maybe*
> *not of his magic. sipho, for your sake today, i ate*
> *like a normal human being. you are a prisoner*
> *here with me until i show signs of improvement. i*
> *had no idea how selfishly i have been thinking*
> *this last while. please keep on eating like you*

have been, and we'll get you home. this whole
idea is ridiculous. i hate it that i hate myself for
eating. so i'll eat for you. you need your mother. i
can only imagine what it has been like for her. to
lose you first, then to find you, and then to not be
able to have you back. please 'scuse me if i've
offended the sangoma etc. around here. i'm torn
between my instincts and the sangoma's idea.
dare i go against him? i don't know, but anna
knows where the village is, where the mother is,
and if i can find out how to get there i might just
have the courage to blow this whole thing.

Joey was washing the stable floors when Emily came down to him at lunch time. She held Sipho on her hip, shielding his head from the sun. His lips were pink on the inside, his face rounder than before. Emily was tired, spent, worn out. Her stomach felt bloated and she frowned. "Hi," she said. "Know where Anna is?"

"Uh, no. No, I don't. How about a 'Hello, Joey, how are you?'"

"Okay," she sighed. "Sorry. So! How are you?"

He dropped the hose pipe and wiped his hands on the pants of his blue dungarees. "I'm fine. Anna's in the kitchen looking for pruning scissors. How's your planting going?"

"Bad. I haven't made even one decent furrow yet. I planted carrots but much too close together," she sighed. "I didn't read the instructions so when they come up I'll have to move them apart."

Joey crept under the paddock fence. He reached out

his hand and touched the top of Sipho's head. His big rough hand looked suddenly quite soft and gentle, and she hitched Sipho up higher on her hip. She licked her lips nervously and squinted up at Joey, blinded for a moment by the sun.

"I've never met anyone like you, Emily," he said, tapping his fingers against his leg. "You're so young, and so ... complicated. You really don't see colour, do you?"

"What do you mean?" She moved Sipho over to her other hip.

"I mean, you're a white kid from the city, but you don't seem to see, you know, that Sipho, well, he's black, and I'm also kind of black, and you don't distinguish, not even for a second. Your face never shows any ... oh, I don't know. Your uncle, he's like that, it goes without saying. But you ... I expected you to be someone quite different, from what Anna said."

"What did she tell you?" Emily's mouth was dry and her heart was racing.

The horses ambled towards them across the paddock. Emily could feel the warm breath from the horse's mouth on her ear as it came up close. She scratched her leg where a mosquito had left a string of white itchy-bites.

"Anna said that you were sheltered. A soft, lost girl with a good heart and a very ordinary mother who had lots of young boyfriends."

"How does she know all that stuff?"

"From your uncle."

"What?"

"Anna and your uncle are very ... close."

"I see," Emily said, and bit her lip. "What else did she tell you?"

"She said that you needed to really learn what it was to have a hard time, so that you wouldn't just be someone with a kind heart, but would have the will to change things. Anna was very aware of you on all your visits here."

Emily felt her head grow hot. She pondered for a moment. When she spoke her voice was soft. "Anna was right," she said.

Joey's face looked puzzled. "No," he said. "That's what I wanted to say. She was wrong. You *have* had a hard time. You don't need to suffer any more. I've seen your art. Your uncle showed me the painting above his bed."

"What painting?"

"Skeletons and pyramids."

It seemed as if Joey wanted to move closer to her. Emily felt her knees weakening. She leant forward until her face was just centimetres from Joey's. Then he bent his head and she looked up into his eyes. "I must go now," she whispered, and stepped away from him. Then she ran as fast as she could to find Anna and to get the blood flowing back into her legs again.

Chapter 10

Light flickered from the candle in the early morning. It shone on a rough sketch Emily had made showing the trail to Sipho's mother's village. There were crosses and circles indicating trees and huts, so that she would know exactly where to find the woman. She studied the map. Anna had seemed slightly suspicious when she had asked again and again for directions to the village. She hoped Anna didn't know what she was planning.

Emily was wide awake and glanced quickly at the luminous hands of her clock. It was four am. She checked the sleeping Sipho and rubbed his back. She didn't want to wake him with any sudden movements. Carefully, she slipped a sheet beneath him and wrapped it around him. "Now," she whispered. "I hope I'll do it right." She dressed herself and picked him up. She used the sheet to bind him tightly to her back, then she opened her bedroom door and walked out into the passage. The floorboards creaked. "Sleep," she whispered, praying that Sipho wouldn't wake.

Outside, the moon was shining. The edge of the horizon was faintly purple. Stones crunched beneath her feet and she held the map tightly in her hand. She had just about memorized the way. She would walk between the two hills at the end of the farm and then follow the river. Stars twinkled and an owl hooted. The insects were loud and seemed excited in the predawn freshness. Emily put her arms behind her and held Sipho closer, feeling how his small stomach pressed up against her as he breathed. "I don't know if this is right," she whispered. "But I have to do it." Eventually she reached the dip between the hills and heard the river. She had never been this far on her own. The woman's face, angry, anguished, haunted Emily. The sky began to grow pink and one by one the stars disappeared. Roosters crowed and spirals of smoke curled up from the valley.

Emily reached the banks of the river. The lush grass had been trampled into a pathway and the water ran alongside it, transparent brown.

The pathway led through a thicket of thorn trees, and Emily bent low to keep them from hurting Sipho. She did not know how much time had passed. As the sun peered over the horizon, fiery red, chasing away a strip of night clouds, she arrived at a fork in the pathway. Emily held her breath and turned, taking the left fork. Sipho awoke and cried, turning his small head, so that she felt his nose in her back.

She untied the sheet and slid him down into her arms. His face was peaceful, his eyes half-open and dreamy. She held him in front of her and carried him up the hill like that.

From the ridge she could see a vast expanse of rolling hills and a small smattering of huts in the green bush below her. The more she looked, the more she saw. Suddenly Emily lost all courage. Her arms began to shake and she felt tears well in her eyes. Sipho lay innocently in her arms, unperturbed, unconcerned. She sat down on the ridge, touching Sipho's cheek with her finger. She gave him his bottle.

A cool breeze lifted the sleeves of Emily's shirt and she felt the sun on the back of her neck. Below her she could see the small breakfast fires. Figures were moving in between the huts. Sipho finished his milk. Emily stood up and held him tightly in her arms. Slowly she began her descent to the village.

She stopped a few metres from the nearest hut. Chickens ran across the sandy patch in front of her. Tears slid down her cheek into her mouth. She couldn't see what she was doing and didn't know what her next step should be. The hut. She had to find out which was the right hut. It all looked so different from how she had pictured it. Somehow there were more huts than she'd expected. Suddenly she noticed someone moving silently between the trees and an outcrop of granite. Emily started forward and tripped. With a cry she held out her arms to protect Sipho. She fell with her elbows and knees in the sand and pinched her eyes tightly together, her hand covering Sipho's head. The sand hurt her and a sharp pain shot through her arms. When she opened her eyes Sipho was beginning to cry, but he was unhurt. She looked up to see a tall woman standing over her. Emily slowly pulled herself to her feet. Her arms ached and she held Sipho shakily. A figure she recognized walked up to the tall woman's side. Emily swallowed. The dress, the eyes, the face. The mother.

The sun shone down. It was a bright morning without any haze. Cooking smells wafted through the air. A skinny goat stood tethered to a fence, bleating heartily into the dawn. Emily had been looking for that fence, but hadn't seen it until now. She stared at the woman and neither of them moved. Emily pointed to Sipho and said the only Zulu word she properly understood. "Sipho."

Sipho. A gift. Tears spilled over her cheeks and she said softly, "I know you don't understand me, but I'm returning this ... gift." She held Sipho out in front of her. The mother, who up until this point had been standing beside the tall woman, took a step towards Emily and her face seemed to crumple. She stretched out her arms and Emily placed Sipho in her trembling hands. Her eyes met Emily's, but only for an instant. As Sipho passed between them, Emily felt as though her insides were being pulled out. She felt her stomach turn in pain as she let go of his small body. The mother directed a loud string of words into the air. Emily realized she was still holding the empty bottle. She held it out but Sipho's mother turned her head away. Sipho belonged in her arms. Slowly the woman began to walk away and Sipho's crying subsided. Just before she vanished behind the trees she turned and looked at Emily. Her eyes were dark and shining. Then she was gone.

Emily was stunned. Her arms throbbed and her head began to ache. The tall woman still stood there. Her face was stern. She frowned at Emily.

"You disobeyed the sangoma," she said.

"Yes," Emily said in a small voice.

"That is the mother of the child."

"I know."

"It is dangerous for you to come here, white girl."

Emily swallowed. Her eyes burnt and she trembled. She looked nervously from the huts to the rocks to the hills to the ridge where she had been sitting just a while before. Perhaps she would not return alive. The breeze stirred the tall woman's skirt. Emily stepped back. She looked behind her at the high ridge she would have to climb. Then the woman's frown lifted. "I will go with you," she said to Emily. "I will take you home."

Emily cleared her throat. She looked at the trees and the branches that crouched low over her head. A flood of relief washed over her. "Thank you," she said.

The woman began to walk silently in the direction of the ridge. Emily wasn't sure if she should follow or not. Suddenly the woman turned and stamped her foot impatiently. "*Woza!*" she said.

The sun was almost midway across the sky. The heat burnt Emily's skin and she held onto Sipho's bottle. Silently she followed the woman. Her head felt as though it might burst. Thorns scratched her legs. The air seemed tense, but the hours passed and nothing happened. Eventually they left the river where they had been walking and Emily recognized the path and knew that they were near the farmhouse.

The first thing she noticed as they neared the veranda was that all the doors and windows of the house were wide open. There was activity. She heard a loud cry. Joey's voice.

"She's here!"

Anna ran out onto the veranda, followed by Joey and Uncle Tim. Joey ran towards her. The tall woman waited. Anna spoke to her in Zulu and she answered. Anna took a deep breath and put her hand to her chest in shock. Joey's warm hand touched Emily's arm.

"Are you all right?"

Emily nodded. "I think you should get her something to drink," she said, pointing at the woman. "She must be exhausted."

what day is it? i don't remember. but it was yesterday that i took sipho back and learned later that i'd walked through an area where there had been fighting. i miss sipho. i can't draw, can't even think, but am eating. anna says that in time something will come from the sangoma, and i should be ready, tho' what it is she cannot (will not) say. the tall woman went back home with a whole lot of fruit from uncle Tim and goat's milk for sipho. there is no way to describe the hollow feeling i have. i was given a gift and didn't realize till too late. i will never be able to draw those skeletons, those ancient egyptian pictures again, that's over. what lies ahead i don't know, only that, ladies and grasshoppers, out here in the cool night on the veranda by candlelight, i see the shadow of a huge giant, and he seems to be looking at me. no, he's winking at me. we're in cahoots, he and i. i have news from the mirror: i've gained weight. so, ladies and grassmen, i am fighting an intense desire to measure my thighs with a tape measure to see how they have expanded.

The vegetable garden was overrun with weeds when Emily finally went to look at it. Carrots had sprouted, but they were so close together that they looked like a single plant. She stared down at the mess in dismay. *Uncle Tim*, she thought, *you have a useless niece*. She bent down and her hair fell over her eyes. Her fingers touched the earth and she tried to weed out some of the carrots. A shadow crossed the sun, and she looked up.

Emily's breath caught in her throat. Her heart raced. She thought she might collapse. Standing confidently in front of her, his strange headdress shining in the sun, was the sangoma. He wrinkled his eyes and Emily smelt a strange odour rising from him. She dropped the carrots and dusted her hands. Through the trees she could just see the roof of the farmhouse. The sangoma was wearing jeans again, but he had decorated the top half of his body with strung beads and a necklace of lion's teeth.

For a moment Emily was speechless. What could she do? She was terrified, and yet she didn't believe that he would actually harm her right there.

"Well," she began softly, her voice trembling. "I don't know if you understand me. I ... am sorry that I disobeyed your instructions. Listen, I don't want to be impolite: I just had to do what I had to do. I just had to return the baby."

"I understand you," his voice boomed into the air. Clouds scudded across the sky. Birds circled overhead. A bug ticked in the grass at Emily's feet and she looked at the sangoma's face, astonished.

"Yes, I speak English. Not often. You did what your soul urged."

A breeze blew the grass so that the soft whisper of wind was all around them like a voice. Emily looked into his eyes. She looked at the torn jeans and the necklace of lion's teeth.

"You are afraid because you disobeyed me."

"Yes," Emily said simply.

The sangoma turned his head away. When he looked back his eyes were closed. He put out his hands. "Put your right hand on my hand," he said.

She did as he'd told her. Her palms were sweaty and his forehead glistened with moisture as though what he was about to do required great effort.

"You have not gone against the desires of the Spirit. You have behaved as you were to do. You have learnt what a mother's pain can be when a child is lost to her. The Great Spirit, who knows all, is in the land. The pulse of the land nourishes us. When you listen to the Great Spirit, you can be healed. Go now, white girl, and dig the earth. You have received gifts from the Earth Mother, but you have also returned them. The boy will live, and he will grow strong. Work the earth and it will feed you. Your illness has passed."

He dropped his hand and looked almost fiercely into her eyes. Then he nodded slowly and walked quietly backwards through the whispering grass until he reached the trees. He turned and passed noiselessly into the green. A strange voiceless breath hung in the air. It was as if all of nature was sighing.

Emily allowed herself to stand there without moving while blood throbbed in her head and in her legs.

She looked at the garden. It was in need of a lot of

attention. One by one she thinned out the carrots and pulled out grass that had begun to encroach on her patch. Her hands ached. She was so busy working that she did not hear the soft footfalls through the grass.

"Such a hard worker," Joey said. "I've been wondering whether you'd forgotten those poor, strangled carrots."

She looked up into Joey's eyes. Then she smiled and wiped her cheek.

"You've just wiped a whole stripe of mud across your face," he laughed and stepped closer. His old leather boots were unlaced. He wasn't wearing socks.

"Where?" she asked.

"Here," he said. His finger gently touched her cheek. "It won't come off," he said and moistened his finger. "No," he said. "That won't work very well either. Come closer."

She did, and his breath was warm on her cheek. When she felt his lips on her skin she closed her eyes. Colours and shadows swam behind her eyelids, and suddenly she moved her head so that their lips met. She leant against him and his arm slipped around her waist.

When she opened her eyes Joey was staring at her. His cheeks were darkly flushed.

"I have to go, you know," she said haltingly. "Back to school, back to my mother."

"I know." He was almost whispering. "Poor Anna, all her children leaving at once."

"Except you," she said.

"Thank goodness for me!" He grinned, but a frown creased his forehead. Overhead, birds circled in the sky. Hadidas. They had a cry that sounded mournful and full of regret. "I should tell you about Anna," he said, and let her go from the circle of his arms. "Amongst the Zulu people she has another name. She's the Earth Mother."

"Earth Mother?"

"That's what they call her. You look so much better. I wanted to tell you but I was afraid. I wanted to tell you that I thought it had a lot to do with you and Anna."

"Thanks," Emily said, and drew a circle in the sand with the tip of her shoe. She couldn't look at Joey. The thought of her other life was looming large.

"I know you'll come back," Joey said. "So don't be sad."

i have missed two weeks of school and can only imagine how much i have fallen behind. i spoke to my mom last night and told her i was coming home. she was quiet and then she said she was glad, really glad. and now there's joey ...

    i can't get the sangoma out of my mind, or out of my nose for that matter. his smell sort of ... lingers. my carrots are coming along. uncle Tim says it's worthwhile and will keep it going until i come BACK *in* APRIL. *i miss sipho. sometimes i think i hear him crying, but of course it isn't. i'm better. i now think that all that stuff about the egyptians and life-after-death and* OTHER *things has truth. I can now be a strong, new Me. I'll be able to look at magazine cover-girls and feel fine. And now, from Me in the Studio, with Big Capital Letters ...* GOODNIGHT.

Emily ate breakfast and Uncle Tim poured her a cup of hot, steaming coffee. Anna flipped pancakes. The kitchen smelt of fried butter and Emily peeled a bit of sunburnt skin from her nose. Anna finished cooking and sat down next to Emily. Joey looked scruffy, as if he hadn't bothered to wash or brush his hair. Anna reached into one of her pockets and took out a small, glass bottle filled with sand.

"This is for you," she said.

Emily took the bottle and looked at the fine grains of sand inside it.

"It's a gift," Anna said. "When you get back to the city, you must grow things. Herbs and plants and flowers. Even if it's in pots. Wherever you can. Put this earth over them and they will grow. And you, Thandiwe, will be better. In time, you will heal completely."

Uncle Tim was smiling at his niece as she took one of Anna's pancakes. He slurped his coffee and patted Joey on the back. "Coming to Durbs?" he asked. Joey shook his head slowly. Emily looked down at her plate. Branches swayed in the breeze outside, and in the paddock the horses were whinnying as if they knew that Emily was leaving.

"Okay, then," Uncle Tim slapped his knee after he'd drained his coffee cup. "We'd best be off. Of course we all have to have Em's promise that she'll be back for the April holidays."

Emily finally had the courage to meet Joey's eyes. She saw the hint of a smile. "'Course," she said. She smiled at Joey and then at Anna and her uncle. "You'll have to tie me to Durban if you don't want me back."

Joey stood next to the car. Uncle Tim closed the front door. Joey took Emily's hand and opened her palm. He put something small and soapy and smooth into it. Lying there was a small, soapstone figure that looked as though it might be crouching on its haunches. Its hands were clasped around its ankles, and it seemed to be asleep. Or perhaps it was simply dreaming. It was the size of Emily's hand. She looked at the precise features, the small stone lips that curved into an enigmatic smile, and the finely detailed closed eyelids.

"It's lovely," Emily said. "Thanks. You're the real artist, Joey. Hey, you know, it looks kind of like ..."

"The Spirit of the Mountain," Joey finished.

"Exactly," she said, and turned it over in her hand.

"I'd better go now," he said. He was about to turn away when Emily stopped him and hugged him.

"See you soon," she said. The front door slammed and Uncle Tim walked across the gravel to the car. "Joey," Emily said. "Look after Anna."

"Don't be crazy. She'll be looking after you and everyone, all the time. You'll see. Even from a distance. Didn't you know she was a healer?"

"A healer?"

"Like the sangoma. She has stronger healing powers than anyone here. Even the sangoma. And he understands."

Uncle Tim was ready to go. The engine was running and Joey took a step back.

"Um, Joey, one last thing," Emily called above the noise. He walked up to the car so he could hear her. "What does the name 'Thandiwe' actually mean?"

Joey smiled and chewed his cheek for a moment,

looking at the distant hills. Then he looked back at her and his face was serious.

"It means, the One who is Loved," he said. "Okay?"

"Okay," she said, and smiled suddenly. "Thanks. See you in April."

Durban appeared slowly through the mist. The buildings emerged like ghosts from some forgotten dream. Emily stared out, accustomed her ears to the hum of traffic, and looked at Uncle Tim.

"Thanks for the ride," she said softly.

"Don't be nervous, it's okay. You'll be fine now."

Late afternoon light filtered through clouds and fog as they drove up the hill. Emily swept her hair out of her eyes and listened to the sea.

I am sitting looking out over the city and Uncle Tim is having tea with my mom in our lounge. I arrived home and noticed that my mom had put a small bunch of flowers on the door handle. When I came in she hugged me. I smelt that she was cooking something spicy. She seemed a bit hesitant, as though she didn't know what to say to me. She said she'd made us both a healthy meal. Uncle Tim laughed and winked at me. "Hey, Meryl," he said. "Don't overdo it now, will you?"

I asked my mom if I could change my room: paint my walls, put flowerpots all along the window, that sort of thing. She nodded. I sneaked a look at her ... she didn't sigh, just nodded again. "Of course," she said. "And, Emily ... I think

*I've been harsh ... no, let me finish. I've misjudged
Anna ... I hope you'll forgive me ..."*

*Yes, my mom said that. Everything has
changed. Somewhere in me there was a clown
who fooled around and kidded herself all her life
that the world was one big joke, that anyone
who dared take things seriously was a washout.
Well, it isn't really like that, you see, crazies and
mentalmen?*

*Now I am going to join them in the lounge
and have some tea.*

Sea fog swallowed up Uncle Tim's car as it vanished
into the morning. Emily stood waving, her arms aching
from the tight hug she had just given him. Her mother
stood at the entrance to their building. Emily took in a
deep breath of sea air and turned around.

"I'd like to do something with you today," her
mother said. "You could choose some plants and art
materials and whatever else you need."

"Okay," Emily said. She thought she might get used
to her mother like this, in time.

A breeze blew Emily's curtains aside. She surveyed her
bedroom wall. She had splattered bright paint across the
white background and used watercolours to make the
dappled effect she was looking for. A fern grew in a pot
next to the colours. Its leaves were huge and green against
her painting. Her whole room was alive. She'd planted
herbs in pots along her windowsill, and on her bedside
table she kept a box of dried rosemary. Emily looked at

the glass bottle Anna had given her. She opened it. Small crystals of sand sprinkled out into her hand and she distributed a quarter of what was in the bottle between all her plants. Then she placed Joey's soapstone figure on her shelf where her books were packed.

I am sitting in the half-dark, looking out of my open window as I write. The moon is full tonight. Tomorrow I go back to school. Tonight is one of those rare, clear nights in Durban. The traffic drones by. There are voices out there. I am holding Anna's jar and looking at the fine granules of sand which seem to shine strangely in the moonlight. I have Joey's sculpture next to me. It's proportions are so exact it almost looks alive — as though it could open its eyes at any moment. I'd better tell him that when I see him in April!

I am looking at the remaining silvery grains in this jar and wondering what magic is inside. Or is it maybe all Anna's love shimmering like that? The truth is that in some way or another, even if only for a short time, Sipho, Joey and I were all Anna's children, and I know that her love, this magic, will carry each of us forward, help us on our way as we grow up under these deep, wide, blue African skies.